D0443200

A JOHN BELLAIRS MYSTERY

FEATURING LEWIS BARNAVELT

The Sign of the Sinister Sorcerer

JOHN BELLAIRS MYSTERY

FEATURING LEWIS BARNAVELT

The Sign of the Sinister Sorcerer

BRAD STRICKLAND

DIAL BOOKS FOR YOUNG READERS

By Brad Strickland
(based on John Bellairs's characters)

The House Where Nobody Lived
The Whistle, the Grave, and the Ghost
The Tower at the End of the World
The Beast under the Wizard's Bridge
The Wrath of the Grinning Ghost
The Specter from the Magician's Museum
The Bell, the Book, and the Spellbinder
The Hand of the Necromancer

Books by John Bellairs
Completed by Brad Strickland

The Doom of the Haunted Opera
The Drum, the Doll, and the Zombie
The Vengeance of the Witch-Finder
The Ghost in the Mirror

Books by John Bellairs

The Mansion in the Mist
The Secret of the Underground Room
The Chessmen of Doom
The Trolley to Yesterday
The Lamp from the Warlock's Tomb
The Eyes of the Killer Robot
The Revenge of the Wizard's Ghost
The Spell of the Sorcerer's Skull
The Dark Secret of Weatherend
The Mummy, the Will, and the Crypt
The Curse of the Blue Figurine
The Treasure of Alpheus Winterborn
The Letter, the Witch, and the Ring
The Figure in the Shadows
The House with a Clock in Its Walls

DIAL BOOKS FOR YOUNG READERS
A division of Penguin Young Readers Group
Published by The Penguin Group
Penguin Group (USA) Inc., 375 Hudson Street, New York, NY 10014, U.S.A.
Penguin Group (Canada), 90 Eglinton Avenue East, Suite 700, Toronto, Ontario,
Canada M4P 2Y3 (a division of Pearson Penguin Canada Inc.)
Penguin Books Ltd, 80 Strand, London WC2R 0RL, England
Penguin Ireland, 25 St. Stephen's Green, Dublin 2, Ireland
(a division of Penguin Books Ltd)
Penguin Group (Australia), 250 Camberwell Road, Camberwell, Victoria 3124,
Australia (a division of Pearson Australia Group Pty Ltd)
Penguin Books India Pvt Ltd, 11 Community Centre, Panchsheel Park,
New Delhi - 110 017, India
Penguin Group (NZ), 67 Apollo Drive, Rosedale, North Shore 0632,
New Zealand (a division of Pearson New Zealand Ltd)
Penguin Books (South Africa) (Pty) Ltd, 24 Sturdee Avenue,
Rosebank, Johannesburg 2196, South Africa
Penguin Books Ltd, Registered Offices: 80 Strand,
London WC2R 0RL, England
Copyright © 2008 by The Estate of John Bellairs

Book designed by Jasmin Rubero
Text set in Cg Cloister
Printed in the U.S.A.

1 3 5 7 9 10 8 6 4 2

Library of Congress Cataloging-in-Publication Data
Strickland, Brad.
The sign of the sinister sorcerer / by Brad Strickland.
p. cm.
"A John Bellairs mystery featuring Lewis Barnavelt."
Summary: In Michigan in the mid-1950s, Lewis Barnavelt is convinced that
the series of accidents he and his uncle are experiencing are the result of
a curse by a mysterious, hooded figure that may be part of his uncle's past.
ISBN 978-0-8037-3151-6
[1. Magic—Fiction. 2. Supernatural—Fiction. 3. Uncles—Fiction.
4. Wizards—Fiction. 5. Witches—Fiction. 6. Orphans—Fiction.
7. Michigan—History—20th century—Fiction. 8. Mystery and detective stories.]
I. Bellairs, John. II. Title.

PZ7.S9166Sig 2008

[Fic]—dc22

2008007698

CHAPTER 1

"LADIES AND GENTLEMEN!" ANNOUNCED Jonathan Barnavelt in a cheerful boom, "for my next trick, I shall require the assistance of a volunteer from the audience! Who wants to be my victim—I mean, my *helper*?"

Sitting in the backyard of 100 High Street with a bunch of his classmates, Lewis Barnavelt couldn't help grinning. It was a June day in the mid-1950s, and in the town of New Zebedee, Michigan, school had just ended. To celebrate, Lewis's uncle Jonathan was throwing a party for Lewis and some of his classmates, and the cheerful, red-haired, bearded, pot-bellied Uncle Jonathan was performing one of his slightly unusual magic acts. Meanwhile, their next-door neighbor, the thin, gray-haired Mrs. Florence Zimmermann, was filling a long picnic table with delicious snacks and refreshments.

In a way, that was funny, because while Lewis's uncle was a real, honest-to-goodness wizard who could create realistic illusions, the friendly, wrinkly-faced Mrs.

1

Zimmermann was a powerful good witch whose magic was far greater than Jonathan Barnavelt's. However, while Lewis's uncle could easily entertain a dozen or so schoolkids, he couldn't cook a decent dish to save his life. Fortunately, Mrs. Zimmermann was not only a sorceress, but also a fabulous cook.

Sitting next to his friend Rose Rita Pottinger, Lewis squirmed around to look hungrily over his shoulder as Mrs. Zimmermann set down a tall, four-layer chocolate-frosted cake, its glossy brown icing making Lewis's mouth water. Then Mrs. Zimmermann, who was wearing one of her light summer dresses (purple, of course, because she loved that color), began to decorate the cake with sweet red maraschino cherries.

Suddenly Rose Rita poked Lewis in the side with her elbow. "Pay attention!" She was a skinny, rather plain girl with long, stringy black hair and big round horn-rimmed glasses, and when she hit you with her sharp elbow, it hurt!

"Okay, okay," mumbled Lewis, and though his stomach was growling, he turned his gaze back toward the temporary stage his uncle had built in the backyard from two-by-fours and plywood. Though he was no expert at carpentry either, Uncle Jonathan had done a pretty good job this time. The platform looked sturdy enough, and Mrs. Zimmermann had draped it with festive red, white, and blue crepe-paper streamers.

"Now, David," said Uncle Jonathan to his shy volunteer, David Keller, one of Lewis's few real friends at school, "I don't know you at all, do I?"

"Huh?" David asked in surprise, and the other dozen or so kids hooted with laughter.

"All right, maybe I know you," said Uncle Jonathan with a wink. "But I'll bet you if you name any object, I can find it in your pockets, or as a last-ditch effort, in mine!" He made a swirling bow. Since Uncle Jonathan, for a change, was not wearing his familiar blue work shirt and khaki wash pants, but a tuxedo (rather tight around his round belly), a black top hat, and a black silk cloak lined with white satin, his bow looked elegant and sweeping.

"Name anything at all," encouraged Uncle Jonathan, holding up his battered old cane dramatically. "Doesn't matter, anything, however outrageous. Think up something you don't believe I'll be able to find in a million years, two months, and eleven days!"

David shifted from foot to foot, his face red with embarrassment at being up in front of everyone. "Uh—an, an e-elephant!" he said finally, stuttering a little.

"An elephant!" shouted Uncle Jonathan. "A tall order! Or at least a great big one! But prestidigitatio pachydermatitis, and behold!" He flourished his crystal-headed cane and waved it like a magic wand.

"Now I say the magic words 'Peanut in a Trunk'! And what is this I find in your shirt pocket?"

David's eyes flew wide as Uncle Jonathan reached into his pocket and pulled out a balled-up gray silk handkerchief. His eyes got wider when Uncle Jonathan dropped the handkerchief softly onto the stage with a grand gesture and waved his cane over it. Something moved around under the silk, looking like a tennis ball. Then it grew larger, as though someone were blowing up a balloon. When Uncle Jonathan bent over and whisked the handkerchief away, everyone yelped in surprise.

A tiny elephant about the size of a white rat was marching around in a circle on the stage. It wore miniature circus trappings: pink ostrich plumes and a red leather harness. As everyone watched, it raised its little trunk and trumpeted, sounding like a kitten playing a kazoo.

"It's not real!" someone exclaimed in derision. "It must be a toy!"

"David, are you trying to pull a fast one on us? Tell us, did you have a toy elephant in your pocket?" demanded Uncle Jonathan, sounding very serious.

"N–no!" replied David. "I didn't even have a r-real one!"

Everyone laughed again at that, but Uncle Jonathan held up his hand for silence. "Who said it wasn't real?"

Lewis and Rose Rita turned around, looking at the

kids behind them. One of them stood instead of sitting among the other kids in folding chairs, and he had his arms crossed and a smart-aleck kind of look on his face. "It's Hal," murmured Rose Rita with a rueful grin.

"Yeah," said Lewis. Hal Everit was a new kid in town, and he had been attending their school for only the last few weeks of class. In that short time, Rose Rita had developed something of a grievance against him because he had edged her out in their history class as the one with the highest average. She had wound up the year with an incredible 98.5 score, but when Hal Everit had transferred in, he had made perfect grades on every quiz and even on the final exam, so his average wound up being 100. As Rose Rita had complained to Lewis, that didn't seem fair. She had been on board for the whole school year, and if she hadn't come down with a bad case of flu back in the winter and missed a whole week of class, she might have had a hundred average too! It was unlike Rose Rita to hold a grudge, but Lewis almost regretted that he had invited Hal.

He had only done it because when he finished handing out the invitations, he suddenly realized that, counting himself and Rose Rita, there would be thirteen kids at the party—thirteen! Sitting in study hall, he had hastily scribbled out another invitation. He was on his way to lunch, trying to think of someone to invite, when Hal caught up with him and said, "Everyone tells me you're having a party."

"Kind of an end-of-school celebration," Lewis had explained.

Hal had sighed deeply. "I wish I could do things like that."

"Why can't you?"

Looking miserable, Hal had shrugged. "New in town," he said in a choked-up kind of voice. "Don't know anybody." He looked away as if embarrassed. "I don't suppose you—you've got room for me?"

And just like that, Lewis had given him the invitation. He felt sorry for Hal, even if Rose Rita wasn't terribly fond of him. Now Lewis hoped that Hal wouldn't be too much of a smart aleck as Uncle Jonathan called him to the stage.

"Step up, step up," Uncle Jonathan was saying to Hal, and he moved through the crowd: a tall, skinny, pale kid with a grave, serious face.

"Right up onto the stage," said Uncle Jonathan in an encouraging tone. "All right, Mr. Doubting Thomas, if that is your real name—"

"It's Hal Everit," said Hal, sounding a little irritable.

"I apologize, Mr. Everit. All righty then, I lift the small elephant like this." Uncle Jonathan bent over and retrieved the tiny animal. He held it in one hand as it waved its trunk. "And I hand you the silk handkerchief that concealed it. Now I will ask you to hold all four corners of the silk together, making a kind of pouch. Two corners in your left hand, two in your right. Yes, that's good. Now, I'm going to place Jumbo Junior here very carefully into the handkerchief. Very well, now bring all the corners together and hold your elephant in a bag, all right?"

Hal did as he was instructed, with David looking on curiously. The dangling silk pouch certainly looked as if it contained something alive. It moved restlessly, bulging and swinging gently.

Uncle Jonathan raised his wand and intoned, "Transformatio columbia livia!" He nodded and then said, "Now, Hal, do you agree that you are holding the miniature elephant in that handkerchief?"

Hal shrugged. "Yeah, I guess so."

"And you think it may not be alive?"

Hal gave him a suspicious look. "It has to be a toy!"

"Very well. Here, I will hold the corners of the handkerchief, and you just reach carefully inside and take out the toy elephant."

"Okay."

Lewis stretched his neck, wondering what his uncle was up to. His magic shows were never the same twice—and he rarely performed them for Lewis's friends, because the kids had a way of talking about the shows that made their unsuspecting parents think that maybe Jonathan Barnavelt was a little more tricky than he seemed. Not very many people in town knew that he was a real sorcerer, and the ones who did were all members of the Capharnaum County Magicians Society.

Carefully, Uncle Jonathan took the corners of the handkerchief and held the pouch slightly open while Hal reached in and felt around. A puzzled look came into the boy's eyes. He reached farther in—and farther—and even farther. The boys and girls watching the show started to giggle and point. Somehow, Hal was leaning way over, his whole arm inside the small pouch of the handkerchief all the way up to the shoulder. It looked impossible, and really it probably was, reflected Lewis. That was his uncle's real magic at work.

It was a warm day, but he shivered a little, remembering an evening some years before when Uncle Jonathan had performed one of his best tricks for Lewis and a boy named Tarby Corrigan. Uncle Jonathan had eclipsed the moon, creating a weird magical darkness that no one outside of the backyard of 100 High Street even noticed. All sorts of strange things had happened in that uncanny darkness—and one of them was that Lewis got the idea to imitate his uncle and try a magic spell that ended disastrously. Ever since, Lewis had felt very timid about trying to do magic himself.

Up on the stage, Uncle Jonathan said encouragingly, "It's in there somewhere. Reach a little deeper. Be gentle, though!"

"Hey!" Hal pulled his arm out. He was holding something gray. But it wasn't an elephant. Looking surprised, Hal opened his hand and a pigeon flew away, cooing in its gurgly birdy voice. Uncle Jonathan shook the handkerchief one, two, three times, and it disappeared with a flash of light.

"Now, what you pulled out of the handkerchief was alive, wasn't it?" asked Uncle Jonathan, stroking his gray-streaked red beard.

Despite his apparent determination to hold on to his skepticism, Hal grinned shyly. "Umm, it *was* alive—but it wasn't an elephant!"

"Very well. Test me. What do you think I couldn't possibly have inside my pockets?"

Hal squinted in thought. "Helium balloons!"

"Let's see!" Uncle Jonathan swirled his cloak dramatically. Everyone oohed as inflated balloons rose from his flapping cape and floated up on the ends of long strings. Each balloon had a word printed on it in squiggly letters: A yellow one said "Umm"; a red one, "but"; a blue one, "it"; a green one, "wasn't"; a purple one, "an"; and an orange one, "elephant."

"Let 'em fly!" shouted Uncle Jonathan, handing the balloons to David.

A laughing David Keller let go of them one at a time. Each balloon flew up about fifty feet and then popped spectacularly. When the "but" balloon burst, it sent up a shower of red sparks; the others produced a cloud of fluffy royal-blue feathers, a puff of lavender smoke, a glittering burst of golden particles, and a noise like a whoopee cushion that made everyone double up in laughter.

Hal chuckled weakly too, but he looked sheepish. Watching the spectacle, Lewis felt a wave of sympathy for the new kid, the outsider. Feeling that people were laughing at you was never any fun.

"It's all right," said Uncle Jonathan, patting his pockets. "I think we got 'em all! Try saying something else to check. Say, uh, 'That was the most fantastic magic trick I ever saw.'"

Making a face that *might* have been a reluctant smile, Hal murmured, "That was the most fantastic magic trick I ever saw." No balloons.

"Why, *thank* you!" responded Uncle Jonathan, giving another impressive bow. He held his hand out, and *pop!* a shiny red top hat appeared in it. He handed this to David, then produced another one, this one bright blue. That one he gave to Hal. "I present you with genuine honorary magician's hats," he said. "Thanks for helping, and if any rabbits come out of those, don't let 'em loose in the house! A big round of applause for my assistants, please!"

Lewis clapped along with everyone else, but just then he noticed something. Or, rather, *someone*, peeking around the corner of the garage, someone dressed very strangely in a maroon-colored hooded robe with the hood pulled up so that Lewis could not see the person's face. He leaned toward Rose Rita. "Who's that?"

"Where?" asked Rose Rita.

Lewis pointed, but found he was aiming his finger at empty air. The robed person had vanished. He blinked, wondering if this was part of Uncle Jonathan's act. It gave him a momentary creepy feeling, though.

Uncle Jonathan said, "Now, I see that Mrs. Zimmermann has just about finished loading up the table with a great feast of goodies that you are going to love, so maybe just one last quick trick. Hmm. Rose Rita, come up here!"

With a grin, Rose Rita popped up from her seat and bounded onto the stage. She knew about Uncle Jonathan's real magic, and she trusted him not to hurt her.

"What's a celebration," asked Uncle Jonathan, "without a few fireworks? Rose Rita, you are going to help me give a magical fireworks show. Please, kids, don't try this at home! You might blow yourselves to kingdom come!"

First Uncle Jonathan produced an empty goldfish bowl. Then he had Rose Rita hold it on top of her head. "Now," he said, "what kind of fireworks do you like best, Rose Rita?"

"Rockets!" she answered at once.

And immediately, to gasps of awe, a dozen rockets shot up out of the empty goldfish bowl. Trailing streamers of colored smoke, they rose higher and higher until finally, with booms and bangs and kerpows, they went off one after the other, bursting into brilliant red, blue, and green stars.

"Someone else!" yelled Uncle Jonathan over the din. "Let's keep it going!"

"A Catherine Wheel!" someone called.

With a tap of the wand, a spinning spiral of sparks rose majestically from the bowl, spraying the audience with silvery fragments and making some of the kids yelp in alarm—but the sparks were not hot at all and evaporated an instant before they touched anything. The whirling wheel of sparks rose higher and higher and finally blew itself apart with a gratifying, stomach-tightening blast.

"Another!" yelled Uncle Jonathan. "Hurry!"

"Roman candles!" yelled Lewis. He liked them because they didn't make much noise at all, and loud noises made him flinch.

Whoosh! Graceful balls of colored fire shot out of the bowl, one right after the other, and then curved back toward the earth, producing red, orange, yellow, green, blue, indigo, and violet smoke trails and leaving a figure in the air that looked like a multicolored symmetrical sketch of a gigantic willow tree. "Now mine!" said Uncle Jonathan. "I want to make Mrs. Zimmermann happy, so—lots and lots of purple smoke!"

Rose Rita shrieked half in alarm, half in glee. A boiling cloud of thick, and yes, very, very purple smoke, erupted from the bowl, spilled out, covered the stage, and poured into the audience. Everyone jumped up, but they had no chance to run, and in an instant the smoke had covered them all completely.

For just a moment, Lewis was lost in purple murk. He held his breath, but when he had to breathe, he found that he couldn't smell the smoke at all, and it didn't choke him the way real smoke would have done. It was just as if he were breathing the fresh air of a summer's afternoon. And a moment later—he was.

Everyone blinked. The smoke had just faded away. And the stage had vanished, along with all the magic props: Uncle Jonathan now stood wearing his familiar old blue shirt, red vest, and tan pants, and he stood not on a stage, but on the somewhat shaggy green grass of the backyard. Next to him, Rose Rita stood uncertainly, her hands still raised over her head to balance a goldfish bowl that was no longer there.

"Thank you!" said Uncle Jonathan, taking one of Rose Rita's hands and leading her in a stage bow, and the kids clapped wildly. A moment later, they were all clustered around him, firing questions and demands at him: "How did you—?" "Was that really a—?" "Will you show us how to—" and over and over, "Do it again!"

Politely but firmly, Uncle Jonathan declined to repeat any of his tricks, and as for explaining them—"Why," he said, "a magician swears an oath of secrecy! If a magician reveals his tricks, his toenails turn blue and play rock and roll music all night long. And I love to sleep too much for that! Come on—let's eat!"

At last! Lewis hurried over to the picnic table and filled up a plate. Soon he, Rose Rita, and David were gobbling their goodies while sitting together on a big beach towel spread on the grass. "That was a g-great show," David sighed happily, his face smudged with chocolate beneath his cardboard top hat.

"And this is great cake," returned Lewis. He wasn't surprised. Mrs. Zimmermann's double-fudge chocolate-frosted cake was one of her specialties, and she made it only once or twice a year.

"Hal's not eating," pointed out Rose Rita.

Lewis glanced over. Hal Everit stood off by himself, his hands in his pockets. He was watching Uncle Jonathan and Mrs. Zimmermann intently, but he didn't move toward the table himself.

"We ought to make him feel more at home," said Rose Rita.

Lewis looked at her in surprise. "I thought you hated his guts!" he said. "He kept you from getting the history medal."

"I don't *hate* him," sniffed Rose Rita. "I just don't think the *school* was very fair about it, that's all. He seems to be a nice enough guy. He took your uncle's ribbing well. Anyway, Hal's new in town, just like you were once, Lewis."

"And m-me too," put in David. His folks had moved into town not too long before, and they didn't know that the place they had bought, a local landmark called the Hawaii House, was haunted by an army of Hawaiian warrior ghosts. The family came close to being taken away by the night marchers, but luckily Lewis and Rose Rita had come to the rescue, along with their two grown-up magician friends.

"So we should make friends with him," finished Rose Rita. "We can show him around this summer."

"I can't," David said. "My mom's taking me to visit my grandparents in Massachusetts all summer l-long. I w-won't be back until August."

"Then the two of us will have to do it," said Rose Rita decidedly. "Maybe he likes baseball. We could play flies and grounders with him, or—"

Lewis sighed. It did no good to argue when Rose Rita took that tone. When she made up her mind to do something, she did it. She was more athletic than he was, and in the summer she was always trying to talk him into grabbing a bat or putting on a baseball glove. And if she wanted him to help make Hal feel welcome—well, he would help, that's all.

"Fine," he said. "But not before I finish this cake!" And he took another bite of the wonderful cake, and the sweet frosting melted in his mouth. By that time he had forgotten all about the phantom-like hooded figure he had glimpsed a few minutes earlier.

THE PARTY TOOK PLACE on a Saturday afternoon. By the following Monday, Lewis had begun to feel as if he were out of school for a good, long stretch. He welcomed the break. Not that he was a bad student, or that he hated school—far from it. Lewis was a sharp kid, very interested in science and math. In fact, he was something of a whiz at astronomy. He and his uncle even had their own telescope, a nifty ten-inch reflector, which meant that instead of using a big lens to peer at the stars and planets, it used a big concave mirror. It let him see the craters on the moon, the white polar caps on orange-red Mars, and the moons of Jupiter, which looked like a row of bright little stars that were usually very close to the planet.

However, after a long school year, Lewis loved nothing better than just to relax for a while, and to him relaxation meant one thing: stretching out in a comfortable place with a tasty snack and a good book to read.

And that was why on that sunny Monday morning Lewis lay comfortably stretched out on a lawn chair, the kind made of aluminum tubing and nylon webbing with a foot part that propped up so he sat with his legs straight out and his back supported. He had placed the chair carefully in the shade of one of the maple trees in the backyard. On a little wrought-iron table beside the chair he had some of his favorite snacks: crisp, buttery crackers spread with pink pimento cheese, a big box of chocolate-covered raisins, and a tall glass of milk. And spread open on his stomach he held an oversized book from his uncle's library.

Lewis really liked poking through the shelves of books in the mansion his uncle owned. The house was ridiculously large for just the two of them, and they mostly lived on the first and second floors. The whole third floor was unused, crammed with furniture hidden under dustcovers. Some rooms practically overflowed with strange odds and ends of various junk that Jonathan Barnavelt had inherited or collected. Lewis had found a stereopticon, a viewer into which you put long sepia-toned double photos that became three-dimensional views when you looked through the eyepieces. One box held thousands of pictures: the Alps with a summer storm coming up behind them, Niagara Falls cascading in summer and frozen like a river of whipped vanilla frosting in the winter, smoky Civil War battlefields with cannon and mules and sometimes dead or wounded soldiers, and many others.

In another room Lewis had found a wheezy pump organ that would still play, though it sounded croupy. And in one of the upstairs rooms he discovered a wall of floor-to-ceiling shelves jam-packed with hundreds of odd old books. They were just the kind he loved, with dusty covers and liver-spotted pages and the heady, spicy aroma that only antique volumes seemed to have.

Just that morning he had pulled down one of these, a tall, thick volume with a blotchy, cracked maroon leather cover and brown, brittle pages dotted with tiny bookworm holes and splotched with brown age spots. The title attracted him at once:

A COMPENDIUM OF CURIOUS BELIEFS
AND SUPERSTITIONS
OF THE BRITONS, SCOTS, AND IRISH
By Theodosius M. Fraser,
B.A., M.A., D.Div. (Oxford), F.R.S.
LONDON
1851

The thought that he was holding a tome more than a hundred years old gave Lewis a pleasant little tingle of anticipation. This was the first book he wanted to read for the summer.

And so, happily stretched out in his lawn chair,

Lewis popped a cheese cracker into his mouth and munched it as he began to read about odd beliefs and practices in old England, Wales, Scotland, and Ireland. The first chapter was all about curious weather omens. Lewis sipped his milk and ate his crackers as he learned about how hares with heavy coats promised a cold winter to come, about how low-flying birds predicted rain and stormy winds, about how sailors should fear a red sky at morning but rejoice at one in the evening, and other superstitions. To tell the truth, it wasn't very exciting, but Lewis fell into the old-fashioned language and drifted along with it in an agreeable kind of daze.

Overhead the green maple leaves fluttered in the morning breezes. Faintly from the street Lewis could hear the occasional sounds of a passing car. A red airplane droned along through a sky dotted with white clouds.

Chapter two made Lewis sit up a little straighter. It was titled rather grimly "Of Harbingers of Death and Disaster."

The chapter began with a discussion of comets as signs of tragedy. It told of the fiery comet seen in England in 1066, the year the Normans invaded and conquered the island. A comet had blazed in the Roman sky the night before Julius Caesar was assassinated in the Forum. Lewis sniffed impatiently. He knew all about comets, and they were nothing to be afraid of. They were icy balls of stone and frozen water whizzing in long, warped orbits about the sun. When they came hurtling in from the depths of space, the sun heated the ice on them and the vapor trailed out behind the comet in what looked like a glowing tail. But he was sure comets didn't really foretell death or disaster. Well, *pretty* sure.

For Lewis was what Rose Rita called a worrywart. His problem was that he had a very active imagination. That was usually good, but too often Lewis used it to picture threats or calamities that had little or no chance of actually happening. Now as he read farther into the book, he hit something that he had often heard people talk about: the Curse of Three.

"Many in this kingdom," Dr. Fraser had written, "firmly hold that deaths and other catastrophes invariably come in threes. If a great personage should die, many an old woman will then solemnly proclaim the death is a sign that within a few days a second will follow, and not until a third celebrated lord or lady dies will the curse be lifted." The chapter went on to mention other types of bad things that happen in threes: earthquakes, storms, losses in war, and many instances of bad luck.

"Hey, Lewis!"

He jumped about a foot, even though he was sitting down, and he choked on the cracker he had been chewing. Lewis scrambled up out of the lawn chair, turning it over, and coughed and sputtered, spraying crumbs.

A contrite-looking Rose Rita stood nearby. "Hey," she said again in a small voice, "I didn't mean to scare you half to death! You okay?" She thumped him on the back.

Lewis gasped for air and took a long drink of milk. "You didn't scare me," he rasped at last. "Crumb just went down the wrong way, that's all."

"You okay now?"

Lewis nodded, but his face felt hot and red. "What are you up to?" he wheezed, trying to make his voice sound normal and not succeeding.

"A bunch of the kids are organizing a baseball game down at the athletic field," said Rose Rita. "It sounds like a lot of good players are going to be there, so I thought you might want to go and join in."

Lewis made a face. Though he was no longer the tubby kid he had been years ago when he first came to New Zebedee, following the tragic death of both of his parents in a car crash, no one would call him athletic. Clumsy, self-conscious, and hesitant, Lewis wasn't much good at sports. Whenever he played, the team leaders always picked him last of all, and at that they would stick him in right field.

"I'm not in the mood," Lewis complained to Rose Rita. "I had my day all planned. I was going to lie here and read my book and enjoy the sunshine."

"But you're in the shade," protested Rose Rita with a laugh. "Oh, come on. At least walk over there

21

with me. If you don't feel like playing, you don't have to. Somebody told me that Mr. Detmeyer will be umpiring."

Lewis gave a resigned shrug. He knew better than to argue with Rose Rita when she fell into a determined mood. And he did like Mr. Detmeyer, a lanky, bald old retired man who hung out at the firehouse and who in his youth had played second base for a minor-league team called the Spiders, out east somewhere. Mr. Detmeyer spun great yarns, and he claimed that he didn't become a major leaguer because during an exhibition game he caught barehanded a sizzling line drive hit by the great Babe Ruth. It had broken every single bone in his right hand, he said, and that ended his hopes for a professional career—"But I put Babe Ruth out!" he always finished with pride.

Even though his playing days were long behind him, Mr. Detmeyer was nuts about baseball and always coached Little League, and if you asked him to come along and umpire at a pickup game, he would gladly go. The kids all liked him, and nobody ever questioned one of his calls.

Lewis grunted, and Rose Rita grinned as if she knew she had persuaded him. "Let me put my stuff away," he said, reaching for his plate, glass, and book. Rose Rita followed him inside. Lewis rinsed the plate and glass in the sink and left them there. He and his uncle were not exactly slobs, but they took their time about doing housework. Later that evening, one of them would wash and the other would dry. Lewis left the book on a shelf in the study, where Uncle Jonathan was chatting with Mrs. Zimmermann. Lewis told him where they were going, and he nodded. "Have fun, you two," he said.

Lewis really didn't mean to eavesdrop, but as he went back into the hall, he heard Mrs. Zimmermann tell his uncle, "I'm only suggesting that you showed off a little too much at the party. You should hear some of the stories that are going around. Even the unimaginative grown-ups are starting to wonder about those fancy fireworks of yours."

Uncle Jonathan chuckled. "Frizzy Wig, parents know their kids exaggerate! Just because you're a real magician with a fancy foreign degree, don't begrudge me a little conjuring show now and again. My old magic teacher once told me, 'You may never be able to do much more than create illusions, but at least you should enjoy that!'"

"Come on, Lewis," said Rose Rita from the front door, and Lewis followed her, hoping that his uncle hadn't made trouble for himself with the party.

Lewis and Rose Rita walked down High Street to where it intersected with Mansion Street, and then down the hill past Rose Rita's house and past the Masonic Temple, and on through town. New Zebedee's buildings were old and varied, with many ornate Victorian houses. The four-block business district was, basically, Main Street, lined with brick stores, most of them boasting high false fronts. At the west end of Main Street the town fountain sprayed a shimmering willow-tree-shaped plume of water from within a circle of white marble columns. Lewis and Rose Rita walked past it, enjoying the cool drift of mist that trailed over them, and then down toward the athletic field, near the Bowl-Mor bowling alley. Long before they got there, Lewis could hear the crack of a baseball bat and the excited yells of kids.

They were a little late. Two teams were already on the field. "Sorry," Lewis said. "It looks like both teams are full. You won't be able to play."

"There'll be other games," Rose Rita said philosophically. "I enjoy watching too. Let's get a good seat." About a dozen kids and even a few older people sat on the bleachers watching the game. Just as Lewis and Rose Rita got to the stands, the pitcher, a kid named Bobby Bielski, whipped a blazing fast one high, hard, and inside, right past the batter, Buzzy Logan. *Smack!* The ball slapped into the catcher's mitt, and from behind the plate Mr. Detmeyer screeched, "Stee-rike thu-ree! You're out o' there!"

The teams changed places, and Rose Rita said, "Hey, look, there's Hal Everit. C'mon, we can sit with him."

Hal sat about three benches up on the far side of the bleachers, all by himself. He leaned forward, his elbows on his knees and his cupped hands supporting his chin. Rose Rita clambered up to sit beside him and said cheerfully, "Hi, Hal. What's the score?"

"Oh, hi, Rose Rita. I thought you'd be here! Nobody has made a score," replied Hal. "Hi, Lewis."

"Hi," said Lewis, sitting down on the other side of Rose Rita. "Why aren't you playing?"

Hal scrunched up his face. "Aw, I'm no good. I can't hit for beans, and I'm too slow to play the field."

"I know how that is," said Lewis. The two exchanged sympathetic smiles.

Buzz Logan's team threw the ball around, warming up, and then Punchy Fain took the mound. Punchy was a tall, skinny kid a year older than Lewis. Punchy had a good curveball and a fair slider. With the crowd chanting, "Batter, batter, batter," he got two strikes and one ball on the first batter, and then the batter looped a long lazy fly to center field, where Buzz trotted backward and easily caught it. "Uh, Lewis, thanks for the invite to your house. Uh, that was a good party," Hal said in a quiet voice, as if he felt embarrassed.

"Thanks," replied Lewis. "I'm glad you enjoyed it."

"Your uncle's pretty neat," added Hal. "You're lucky. My dad ran off an' left Mom and me a couple of years ago, and then she lost her job, and we had to move from a nice house to a crummy one—bad things happen in threes, they say. Anyhow, I wish I had an uncle."

Feeling a little shudder at that thought again—bad

things happening in threes—Lewis nodded and murmured, "He's great."

"Mrs. Zimmermann had a little to do with it too," put in Rose Rita loyally. "The refreshments were scrumptious."

"But the magic was the best," returned Hal, almost in a whisper.

A nervous Lewis darted a warning glance toward Rose Rita. Gossip about fireworks aside, people in town didn't much bother wondering about Jonathan, who had inherited a pile of money from his grandfather. As Jonathan had cheerfully explained more than once, when an ordinary person acts funny, people think he's crazy. But when someone with money acts funny, people smile and call him eccentric.

As for Mrs. Zimmermann, people did gossip a bit about her. She was a retired schoolteacher who always wore purple and drove a purple car, and she had a way of showing up almost exactly when people needed help. Some people called her an oddball, but almost everyone in town liked her. Still, very few of them knew that she was an accomplished sorceress and an expert on magical talismans and amulets, and she liked to keep those facts secret.

Hal had produced a yellow pencil from his pocket. He waved it like a baton. "Presto! Alakazam! I'd like to learn how to do magic," he said. "Maybe your uncle could teach us—all three of us."

Lewis realized that Hal was imagining the pencil as a magic wand. He began to feel uncomfortable. "Well, you can get books and special card decks and stuff," he said, trying to sound casual and unconcerned.

"They sell different magic kits at the Magician's Museum in town," added Rose Rita.

"No, not just tricks from a kit," whispered Hal impatiently. He leaned sideways, and his voice sank to a soft, insistent level. "Haven't you ever read about people like Count Cagliostro, or the Order of the Golden Circle, or Prospero and Roger Bacon? I mean real magic. Spells. Sorcery."

Lewis laughed, hoping that it sounded disbelieving and just the smallest bit scornful. "But that's not real. Magic like that is stuff you find in storybooks, that's all."

Hal gave him a long sideways look and a little knowing smile. "I saw what your uncle was doing with his cane. You can't tell me that was all just smoke and mirrors and a bunch of tricks you can buy in the store!" He swept his yellow pencil around and around and then pointed it at Lewis.

Crack!

"Look out!" shouted Rose Rita.

Too late. Lewis had been staring at Hal. He jerked his head around exactly at the moment when the high foul ball came hurtling down. He caught just a glimpse of the ball, and time seemed to slow down, and then the baseball struck him hard on the forehead and right between the eyes. The world flashed in a sickening flare of brilliant yellow, and then everything faded to black.

When Lewis opened his eyes again, he found himself lying on the grass, with everyone crowded around him. "What happened?" he asked, and his voice sounded funny even to him. His ears were ringing and he had a terrific headache.

"Lie still, son," said Mr. Detmeyer, pushing down on Lewis's left shoulder. "You got clocked a good 'un by a foul ball. Don't stir around, now, and it'll be okay. Somebody's gone to get the doctor to come check you out."

Lewis groaned. His head throbbed horribly. His nose felt funny too, as if it were swollen and all clogged up. He struggled not to cry, and he didn't sob out loud, but he still felt tears leaking out of the corners of his eyes and creeping down to his temples, first warm, then cold.

After what felt like hours, Dr. Humphries pushed through the crowd, swinging his rattling black leather doctor's bag and calling, "Let me through, let me through here!" His deep, musical voice sounded like a bass viol. Even though he was wearing a good black suit, he knelt in the grass beside Lewis and clucked his tongue. "Great day in the morning, Lewis! You've been pounding in fence posts with your forehead again! You are going to have two beautiful shiners, my boy. Too bad the town mascot isn't a raccoon—you'd be in line for the job! Look here and tell me how many fingers I'm holding up."

"Three," said Lewis, and the doctor nodded. His nose tingled. "Id by nothe broken?" he asked.

"Nope, your schnozz is bloody but unbowed." The doctor leaned in close and peered first in Lewis's right eye, then in his left. Then he turned on a little penlight and moved it around, telling Lewis to follow it with his eyes. Grunting in satisfaction at last, the doctor put the penlight back in his pocket and said, "Looks like you caught it just high enough to protect your eyes and nose, but too low to protect your noggin. You have a lumpus on the bumpus, but your pupils look normal. I think you'll be all right after a few days. Miserable in the meantime, but all right in the end!" He turned away and said, "Rose Rita, please run back to the drugstore and call Jonathan. I think Lewis needs to get home and put some ice on this goose egg he's wearing, and he most definitely will not feel like walking just at the moment."

The doctor wiped Lewis's lips and chin with some gauze dampened in something that smelled like witch hazel, then helped him sit up. Sharp red pain flashed through his head, and a groaning Lewis slumped with his head down, feeling sick. Soon Rose Rita came running back, out of breath, and not long afterward,

29

Uncle Jonathan's big old antique car, a long black 1935 Muggins Simoon, turned off the street and into the gravel parking area so fast that it sent up a cloud of dust and a spray of loose pebbles. The car slid to a dusty stop, and Uncle Jonathan, pale in the sunlight, came running over, his red hair and beard flying in the breeze.

"Don't bust a blood vessel, Jonathan. Lewis is all right," said Dr. Humphries. "Fortunately, Rose Rita had the presence of mind to come and get me. I know it looks terrible, but this kind of thing happens all the time, and pretty nearly a hundred percent of the victims recover with no complications. Take this boy home, put an ice pack on his head, and make sure he doesn't start having hullabaloosions or talking in Esperanto. Keep him awake until tonight. Call me right away if he has any suspicious symptoms. You have aspirin?"

"Sure," said Uncle Jonathan.

"Follow the dosage. Lewis will be all right in a few days. Meanwhile, I recommend rest and relaxation." He patted Lewis on the shoulder in a friendly way. "Go lie in a lawn chair and read a good book!"

Lewis gave Rose Rita a meaningful glance. "That'd judt whad I plan to do," he said in a voice that sounded as if he had a terrible head cold.

Uncle Jonathan and Rose Rita helped him to the car, and they all climbed in. Then for the first time,

Lewis noticed that his shirtfront showed streaks of bright red blood. From his nose, he guessed.

He wished he hadn't looked down. The sight of blood made him feel sick. Especially when the blood was his own.

CHAPTER 3

As Dr. Humphries predicted, by the next morning Lewis felt a lot better, but he had two spectacular black eyes, and his eyelids had turned a strange purply-pink and had puffed up so that he gazed at the world through two narrow slits. His nose still felt stuffy, and when he blew it, crusted blood came out. It was disgusting, but fascinating enough so that he blew his nose three or four times just to see how much he could produce. Uncle Jonathan brought up the ice pack, filled with ice that he had crushed by wrapping cubes in a cloth and beating them with a hammer, and he insisted that Lewis hold it to his eyes for several minutes.

At nine Mrs. Zimmermann came over and prepared breakfast, and she and Uncle Jonathan served it to Lewis in bed. Despite his discomfort and his still-aching head, Lewis grinned at the sight of a neat stack of waffles, dripping with butter and half-hidden under a mound of glazed strawberries and a generous dollop of whipped cream. And Mrs. Zimmermann had made tasty sausage links too, and the tray held orange juice and a big glass of milk. "Thanks," said Lewis, and he sat up in bed, his back propped against two pillows, and wolfed down the breakfast.

Mrs. Zimmermann settled in a chair near his bed and her wrinkly, friendly face split into a satisfied smile. "You are most welcome. And judging from the fact that you're eating like a starving lumberjack, I suppose you really aren't as badly injured as Weird Beard here led me to believe. From the story he told of your accident, I really expected to find you bandaged from head to toe, wrapped up like the mummies in the Museum of Natural History!"

Behind her stood Uncle Jonathan, wearing his red vest. He hooked his thumbs in the pockets, spread his other fingers on either side of his pot belly, and grumbled, "Oh my stars and garters, it was bad enough, Florence! You just try stopping a high fly ball with your forehead sometime and see how you feel the next day! But Lewis will stay in bed and rest for as long as he wants today, and maybe this afternoon or tomorrow he'll feel like getting up and about. Want me to bring the radio in for you, Lewis?"

Lewis patted his lips with his napkin and stifled a very satisfied burp. "No, but you could bring me a book I was reading. I left it on a shelf down in the study. It's a big old one, bound in reddish-purple leather, and it's about superstitions. It's on the shelf to the left of the door, not shelved but just lying on its side."

Uncle Jonathan gave him a salute. "Mission accepted. I'll be right back."

Mrs. Zimmermann smiled sadly at Lewis and shook her head, dislodging a tendril of her untidy gray hair so that it fell from the bun on the back of her head and dangled down by her cheek. "Your poor swollen face! Those two black eyes make you look very different. Can you see all right? Will you be able to read?"

"I can see fine," said Lewis. "Nothing is blurry or anything. It's like I'm peeking between my fingers or something, though. How long will it take for the purple to go away?"

With a grin, Mrs. Zimmermann said, "Well, as a rule I like purple, but I understand why you want to get rid of that particular coloration as fast as possible. A bruise is caused by blood that leaks out of the capillaries when you get an injury. It fades as your body reabsorbs the blood. I'd guess you have at least two weeks before you're back to normal again."

Lewis made a face. "Great."

Mrs. Zimmermann gathered up the tray with its dirty dishes. "Well, you can speed the healing along if you use the ice pack regularly and don't overtire yourself, Lewis. Drink plenty of fluids and rest as much as you can for the next day or two."

Lewis promised that he would, and soon after that Uncle Jonathan returned with the big volume of superstitions. "Here you are," he said, handing it over. He reached to switch on Lewis's bedside reading lamp and continued, "Now, I've put a little bell on the table beside your bed, next to the ice pack there. And I've put a little spell on the little bell. If you need me to bring you anything or do anything for you, just give it a good jangle. Want to try it out?"

"Sure," said Lewis. He picked up the bell. It was like a miniature version of an old-fashioned teacher's desk bell, with a black wooden handle and a small shiny metal body about the size of a golf ball. Lewis held the handle tight and shook it. Instead of the tiny tinkle he expected, he got a resounding *gonnnnng!* He tried it again and heard an antique car horn's *ah-OO-gah!* and then the gruff warning bark of a big dog. Lewis chuckled in appreciative surprise. "It's swell."

"And though it doesn't seem particularly loud in here, because I didn't want the noise to bother your poor aching head, the spell means that I will hear it no matter where I am," promised Uncle Jonathan. "So if you need anything, just ring for Jeeves. Of course Jeeves won't come, but I'll be up here in a flash!"

"Umm," Lewis said hesitantly. "I did sort of want to ask you something."

"Shoot!" said his uncle.

Lewis didn't meet his eyes. He didn't want his

uncle to know that he had been eavesdropping. "Well," he said, "I wonder if maybe you made too big a deal out of those—those fireworks and all at the party. People in town are talking about them."

Uncle Jonathan sighed. "I've heard about that already," he said with a glance at Mrs. Zimmermann, who stood silently holding the tray. "If the FBI shows up at our door to investigate, Lewis, I will have a few plain old conjuring tricks to show them. Don't worry. This will blow over."

"Maybe you shouldn't do real magic for the kids, though," said Lewis. "I mean magic like, uh, Count Cagliostro or the, uh, Golden Circle—"

Mrs. Zimmermann's eyebrows rose. "Heavens, Lewis! Where did you hear those names?"

"I think I read them or something," replied Lewis. "I don't know much about them, though."

"Cagliostro was a scoundrel," said his uncle firmly. "He was a fellow who roamed around Europe in the eighteenth century, swindling people out of money and claiming to be a magician. The Order of the Golden Circle was a brotherhood—"

Mrs. Zimmermann cleared her throat loudly.

"—and sisterhood," added Uncle Jonathan, "of magicians who started out devoting themselves just to the study of magic but ended up bickering, brawling, and falling to pieces. It was pretty much gone by the time I started to study magic, though my teacher had at one time been a member of it."

"You've never told me about your magic teacher," said Lewis.

"Haven't I?" said Uncle Jonathan, seeming surprised. "Well, it's no deep dark secret. One of the teachers at my college dabbled in magic as a kind of hobby, and he took two of us students in and gave us lessons now and then, that's all."

"The Rule of Three," murmured Mrs. Zimmermann.

Three. Again. "What's that?" asked Lewis, not sure he wanted to know.

Uncle Jonathan shrugged. "Something that a lot of magicians believe in. If you're learning magic, you can try to do it all by yourself, or you can be an apprentice to a sorcerer. But if it's a real old-fashioned magic teacher you're dealing with, he or she will almost always want two apprentices at once— the Rule of Three. Magic is better when it's balanced, and three people, a teacher and two students, balance each other like a tripod."

"My first magic teacher believed in it," said Mrs. Zimmermann. "Granny Weatherby taught one of her nieces and me the basics of magic at the same time."

"Now," said Uncle Jonathan, "are you all settled in? Need anything else? All right, then, Florence and I will leave you alone now. I remember that time when I conked my noggin, all I wanted was to be left in peace, and Frizzy Wig here was determined to be at my side every minute. I couldn't get rid of her!"

"I don't remember you complaining about that at the time! Anyway, you ate my cooking and didn't complain," teased Mrs. Zimmermann tartly. They went out, still squabbling good-naturedly, and Lewis picked up his book. With a frown, he turned to the index, and sure enough, there was an entry for the Rule of Three.

And only a second later, he sat up in bed, his heart pounding hard. The first few paragraphs he read sounded truly alarming:

> Among those who fancied themselves prac-
> titioners of witchcraft, the Rule of Three dic-
> tated that every magician in training had to
> join with a teacher and another student; for
> all too often, one of the students became a
> thoroughly evil wizard, and then the other
> two had to join forces to destroy the third.
> Three in witchcraft and wizardry is a number
> of balance and protection, and in any group of
> three, each member is linked to the other two,
> so that if an evil wizard should sorcerously
> attack his teacher or his fellow student, the
> third will instantly feel the attack and rush to
> the rescue.
>
> Similarly, often evil and malign sorcer-
> ers are said to work in groups of three, for
> the number adds more force to their wicked
> enchantments.

Lewis turned a page and found himself staring at a horrible illustration, not a photograph but an engraving. It showed a woman tied at a stake, with a crowd pressing in around her. She stood on a jumbled pile of wood, and it was afire. Flames were licking at her body, and her eyes had rolled up in agony.

"The first witch burned in the first persecution of magicians of the fifteenth century," the caption read. "By the end of the summer, three in all had been so dealt with, and after the death of the third, the magical disturbances ended."

Lewis grimaced. He didn't really want to look at the poor woman's face, locked in an expression of intense suffering, but he couldn't help himself. He swallowed hard, imagining her terror as she struggled against her bonds, with the flames crackling, the smoke rising, and the people mocking her and making fun of—

Not able to stand it, Lewis turned back to the index, but there was no mention of any Golden Circle, nor of Cagliostro. He had forgotten the names of the other two people Hal had mentioned. Lewis put the book on his bedside table and lay back puzzling over the significance of the number three.

It seemed weird and strange to Lewis. Why was three a number of balance? Why not four, or five? He reached for the book again, but in it he found only a couple of very short passages about magicians, and these explained very little. Lewis went back to superstitions about death—three again!—and read an unsettling tale about a Captain Lewis Nevins, a member of the British Army during the Peninsular Campaign against Napoleon back in the early 1800s. Nevins had been cursed by an old man who had "an evil eye." The next day, during a game of cricket, Nevins had been struck by a ball and had told his friends he would die because of the curse, and within one day he did suffer three accidents: first being struck by the ball, then being wounded in the elbow when a musket discharged while a man was cleaning it, and finally dying horribly in a fall down a flight of stairs.

Lewis felt his stomach flutter with sick apprehension. This British Army officer, whose first name was the same as his, had predicted his own death! Well, maybe not exactly, but something close to it. And even worse, Captain Nevins's first injury was almost precisely what had happened to Lewis! A cricket ball wasn't that much different from a baseball. For a panicky moment, he wondered what troubles would lie in store for him in the next hours: a broken arm, a fever, a fatal accident—"Oh, get a grip!" he told himself angrily and aloud.

For he really hated being such a worrywart, but worrying and fretting were as much a part of Lewis as his sandy blond hair or the funny crook in his little toes. He knew very well that Captain Nevins's first name being the same as his own was nothing more than a coincidence. Lewis tried to reassure himself that accidents like the ones in the book were flukes. They could have happened at any old time. Just because the superstitious officer took the cricket ball as a sign—

But, a treacherous little voice inside him insinuated, it *had* been a sign, hadn't it? According to the book, the captain had been sure that the first accident would be followed by two others, and that each would be worse than the one before. His apprehensions had turned out to be true: A broken arm was certainly worse than a bump on the head. And the third misfortune had killed him.

Lewis had dropped his book facedown on the bedcover. Now he picked it up again and skimmed several pages. Then he turned to the index, looking for "antidotes" and "counter-spells" and "good luck" and such terms, but nothing that he found under these headings reassured him much. Oh, the author mentioned a ton of good-luck charms, from four-leafed clovers to rabbits' feet, and quite a few cheerful omens of good fortune to come, but he didn't seem to say a single word about how to avoid a series of catastrophes once they had begun to occur.

A concerned Rose Rita came over to visit at about three that afternoon and Lewis came downstairs in his pajamas and baggy brown robe. After Rose Rita had tutted over his black eyes, the two of them sat in the study and played chess with the set of men that Uncle Jonathan had enchanted. Lewis liked it because Uncle Jonathan claimed the pieces had been carved by a blind German artist in the sixteenth century, and indeed the chessmen looked really old. They were carved from two different kinds of wood, with the white men being a creamy, buttery color and the black side a ruddy, deep mahogany. Their contours had been worn smooth from years and years of play.

The magic spell that Uncle Jonathan had cast on them gave the chess pieces crabby, fluty little voices, and they complained constantly about how they were being moved. A pawn would grumble, "Oh, sure, move me out where I can be captured! What about the bishop's pawn, huh? He's just standing there, not doing anything, the lazy bum! Use him instead!" When a knight captured another piece, it just about went crazy in a high-pitched voice of excited, frenzied triumph: "Ho, down with thee, thou blaggardly varlet! Thou hast met thy master, I trow! Victory is mine! O frabjous day! Calloo! Callay!" And all through a game, both queens kept droning in displeased, flat, vinegary voices, "We are *not* amused."

As a rule, Lewis played a cunning game of chess. He had a knack of figuring out moves well in advance and he loved to build a strategy that his opponent wouldn't recognize until it was too late to avoid a slowly constructed trap. Rose Rita was pretty good herself, but she often got distracted talking about other things, so sometimes she made careless little mistakes that Lewis was sure to pounce on.

As Lewis set up the board for their game, Rose Rita kept darting glances at his face. "You look awful," she told Lewis cheerfully. "Like you've been in a fistfight with Rocky Marciano." Lewis just grunted. Rocky Marciano was a world-champion heavyweight boxer. Rose Rita tilted her head and asked, "Does it still hurt?"

Lewis shrugged. "Kind of a dull headache, that's all. But I've taken some aspirin for that. Dr. Humphries came by again right after lunch, and he says that since I don't have any ringing in my ears and no blurred or double vision, I probably don't have a concussion, so I'll be okay. Here, choose one." He held out his fists, and Rose Rita picked his right one. He opened his hand to reveal a white pawn. Rose Rita would play the white side in the game, meaning she got to move first, and he would play black.

"You know, in the movies when someone gets hit on the head he always develops amnesia," said Rose Rita as she shoved her queen's pawn forward two squares, to its grouchy mutters of protest. She ignored the pawn's mosquito-like whining about being sent forward to battle and asked Lewis, "You don't have amnesia, do you? How are you at remembering stuff?"

Lewis moved a squabbling pawn forward. "I remember stuff fine," he said, watching as Rose Rita moved another man. "I remember you yelled for me to look out, just *after* the nick of time."

"I'm really sorry," said Rose Rita, looking miserable.

With a shrug, Lewis said, "I'm not blaming you. If I hadn't looked up, I probably would have been conked on the top of the head, and that might have been worse. Anyway, when you yelled, I looked up and saw the ball about a foot from my face right before it smacked me. Everything turned yellow and then black. Thanks for going to get the doctor, by the way." Lewis made his move, and then Rose Rita had moved again, giving Lewis a chance to maneuver his queen out to a safe position, where it threatened one of Rose Rita's bishops.

"I ran pretty fast," said Rose Rita, seeing the trap that Lewis was working on and moving her bishop out of danger. It squeaked, "Praise be! For this fair rescue we give humble thanks."

"I guess Hal Everit just ran, period," said Lewis, bending forward to study the board. "Anyhow, I didn't see him when I came to."

"Well, the whole thing probably scared him," said Rose Rita. "It happened so suddenly, it shocked everybody. I mean, one second Hal was sitting there talking to you and then the next, blam! The ball smacked into your head, and you fell right off the bleachers and flat on your back in the grass. I jumped down to see if you were all right, and you were out cold. You looked pretty bad, you know, with blood dribbling out of your nose, down your chin and onto your shirt. I guess Hal took off about the same time I did. Anyway, he was long gone by the time Dr. Humphries drove us over. Don't blame Hal, Lewis. Some people are very squeamish about blood."

"About the last thing I remember before getting hit was him waving that stupid yellow pencil in my face," muttered Lewis. "And asking us about Uncle Jonathan's magic. I know Mrs. Zimmermann's been worried that people are talking about those magic fireworks all over town."

"They'll forget soon enough," Rose Rita assured him. "Just wait until something new comes along— some young couple will elope, or a deacon of a church will get arrested for drunk driving, and they'll have something else to gossip about."

"But Hal's interested in magic, so we're going to have to be careful around him. It was bad enough when David found out what Uncle Jonathan and Mrs. Zimmermann could do."

"David sort of had to find out about them," she told Lewis in a reasonable tone. "Otherwise, the evil spirits haunting his house would have killed him and his whole family. Oh, no!" She had just noticed that in relocating her bishop, she had made a very bad move.

Lewis swept his rook forward, capturing a pawn.

The rook cawed in triumph, like an exulting crow, and the captured pawn moaned, "Man, sometimes life just stinks!" The move left the rook poised with Rose Rita's king threatened. All she could do was to move her king one square, and that was just prolonging the agony, because in the next move Lewis could trap it in checkmate. "I resign," she said, sounding irritated with her own bad judgment.

Her king moaned, "Uneasy lies the head that wears the crown! Look out, everyone, I'm falling down!" and tipped itself over.

The two friends had a snack, and then Lewis walked Rose Rita to the front door. They glanced in the hall mirror, the one that was set in a coatrack that had pegs for hats and coats and a little bench in front. Like many things in the Barnavelt house, the mirror carried an enchantment. The glass sometimes reflected your face, but often it showed strange, faraway, and even other-worldly scenes. And sometimes Chicago radio station WGN faintly came in on it, but Lewis's uncle had told him that wasn't magic. The beveled edges of the glass, he claimed, created a kind of primitive crystal radio receiver.

Rose Rita said, "That's kind of spooky-looking." The mirror today showed a moonlit clearing in a dark wood. It seemed to be a winter scene—at least, the grass looked stiff and white with frost in an irregular rounded clearing in a gloomy and foreboding forest. In the background, dozens of tall, thick evergreen trees brooded, their trunks dim gray streaks, their tops deep dark green cones. An eerie kind of pale fog wove in and out of the trees in thin, glutinous-looking streamers. And as Lewis stared, a strange figure melted out of the darkness. It seemed to be a tall man wearing a maroon robe with a head covering like a monk's hood concealing his face.

"Hey," said Lewis, "that guy looks familiar. I think I saw him once before!"

"What guy?" asked Rose Rita, peering through her round glasses.

Lewis swallowed hard, remembering that he had seen the same person, or one dressed just like this, at the corner of the garage during the party. The robed person in the mirror paced around in the circular clearing, then faced them, spreading his arms dramatically.

"I can't see anything but—" began Rose Rita, but a worried Lewis shushed her and leaned close, peering into the mirror with a rising feeling of dread in the pit of his stomach.

Lewis squinted, trying to decide whether the shrouded creature was holding a wand. It looked as though he had one in his right hand, but the image was dim and dark, and the figure was really very tiny. Then the right arm moved, and with a quick slash the hooded form began to leave a trail of fire in the dark air.

Lewis gasped.

The phantom shape had quickly stepped back into the shadows and had vanished.

But floating in midair was the fiery figure his hand had traced.

It was a glowing, shimmering golden orange numeral:

CHAPTER 4

"IT WAS A THREE!" insisted Lewis hotly.

"It was just an orange squiggly line," returned Rose Rita. "And I didn't see a little man at all. I saw a drifting, maroony-grayish sort of blob, and then it jerked, and there was an orange squiggle in the air for a second, and then the mirror went back to normal."

The mirror was undeniably back to normal now. Lewis could see his face with its purple raccoon-eyes staring back at him. He swallowed hard and insisted, "I saw a man in a robe! Well, a person in a robe, anyway—I suppose it could have been a tall woman. It looked like a medieval monk, with the hood up and everything."

Rose Rita looked at him strangely. "A monk?"

Lewis went on, "And I'm pretty sure the person was holding a—a wand, or anyway, a thin kind of stick or something. That's what he or she used to draw the number three in the air!"

Rose Rita shook her head, her expression thoughtful but unconvinced. "I don't know. I couldn't see anything at all very clearly, to tell you the truth. It was dark and blurred."

"Besides," muttered Lewis, almost as if Rose Rita hadn't even spoken, "I saw someone in a robe just like that one last Saturday at the party. It was while Uncle Jonathan was doing his magic. Whoever it was must've ducked right back around the corner of the garage at the same time I noticed him standing there, because one moment he was there and the next—what's the matter?"

Rose Rita was biting her bottom lip and looking uncomfortable. "Long maroon robe?" she asked. "Tied at the waist with a belt that looked like a rope? Sort of a skinny person, maybe about as tall as Mr. Morgan, the basketball coach at school? Hood up so you couldn't see the person's face?"

Lewis blinked. "I don't remember about any kind of belt, but yes, the hood had been pulled up over the person's head. Why?"

Frowning in concentration, Rose Rita said, "I thought I saw someone like that yesterday, right after you got conked by the foul ball."

"Wh-what?"

Rose Rita shrugged. "I'm not even sure. It was just a glimpse. It happened when I was running to get Dr. Humphries, and up at the street I looked back over my shoulder at the field. Under the trees down at the far end, close to the railroad tracks, I sort of thought I saw someone in a monk's robe, just standing there quietly. But gosh, that's about a hundred yards past the baseball diamond! At that distance it might have been a tree stump, for all I know. I haven't had my glasses changed this year, and—"

"Three times." Lewis's throat was dry. "The party, the mirror, the athletic field—he's been seen three times! Come on, I think we'd better tell Uncle Jonathan."

His uncle was in the dining room, paying the Barnavelt household bills. He had his checkbook out, his prized gold fountain pen in his hand, a stack of envelopes and a sheet of purple three-cent stamps at the ready, and nearby stood a Chinese abacus that he used to add and subtract faster than Lewis could with paper and pencil. As the two came in, he looked up and smiled. "How did the great chess tournament end?" he asked. "Did Rose Rita take you to the cleaners, Lewis? You look down in the dumps!"

"No, I won," replied Lewis. "But listen to this." He and Rose Rita pulled chairs out for themselves, and they quickly told him about the reflection in the mirror and about the hooded figure—or figures, perhaps—that they thought they had seen.

To Lewis's relief, Uncle Jonathan listened gravely to them, never once interrupting and never making noises of disbelief. Though Uncle Jonathan sometimes confessed that he worried about raising Lewis—

"An old bachelor like me simply doesn't know much about kids," he had said once—Lewis really appreciated the way his uncle never talked down to him or treated him like a child.

When Rose Rita and Lewis finished their story, Uncle Jonathan thoughtfully dug a curved pipe from his shirt pocket. He no longer smoked, but sometimes when he was in a thoughtful mood, he liked to hold the pipe between his teeth. It helped him ponder, he said, and the old briar British Bulldog pipe was his favorite thinking aid because it looked like Sherlock Holmes's pipe.

For a minute or so he just sat there clenching the pipe in his teeth, and then he murmured, "Hum. And also ah, and other assorted expressions of mild puzzlement." He tore a sheet of paper from the pad where he kept track of the monthly budget and passed it together with a pencil to Lewis. "Draw this mysterious character for me. Don't worry if you can't make it look like a van Gogh or a Picasso! It doesn't have to be a perfect sketch. Just show me the general shape."

Lewis took the pencil and drew a fairly formless figure, with the heavy robe billowing down on both sides, and then he added the hood and shaded in the place where the face should have been. "Is this like what you saw?" Lewis asked Rose Rita.

She shook her head. "I can't tell! What I glimpsed was really far away. I mean, it was tiny in the distance! But it might be. Except I think the robe was sort of cinched in by a belt. I don't know why, but I think the belt might have been made out of a piece of dark rope."

Uncle Jonathan studied the sketch and stroked his beard thoughtfully. He absently picked up the pencil and sketched in a belt around the drawing's middle. Then he took the pipe out of his mouth and shook his head. "This does look reminiscent of something, but—well, no, it couldn't be. That was years and years ago. Hmm."

He put the paper down and drummed his fingers on it. "Well, Lewis, I can tell you this much: I don't think you saw a ghost! It might have been some joker who looked at the calendar wrong and thought Halloween was coming five months early. Or it could be a deranged TV weatherman wearing a maroon raincoat because he's sure we're due for a frog-drowning downpour. But for what it's worth, I don't think any ghoulies, ghosties, or long-leggity beasties have been creeping around Castle Barnavelt."

"What did you mean about something years and years ago?" insisted Lewis.

His uncle chuckled. "It's just that when I was a much younger fellow than I am now, some magicians thought you had to dress up in robes like that to perform magic properly. I've worn a robe in my time too, but take it from me, it isn't absolutely necessary. Not much is—though I'll cheerfully admit that a magician is about a dozen times more powerful when equipped with a wand he or she can rely on, attuned to that magician's special powers. Still, an accomplished magician can scrape by without a wand in an emergency. Florence is good enough to be able to cast a magical whammy just using her fingertips! So as far as being worrisome, the robe is more curious than threatening; that's all I'm saying."

"What about the figure Lewis saw in the mirror?" asked Rose Rita.

Uncle Jonathan seemed a little uncomfortable, Lewis thought, but he said, "That fool looking glass shows strange things all the time. There's a good chance that the blobby maroon thing you saw was something entirely different from a hooded human. I'd chalk it up to coincidence, if I were you, and try to forget about it."

"That's what I think too," added Rose Rita with a nervous sort of sideways glance at Lewis.

But Lewis wasn't so sure. He knew what Rose Rita must be thinking: There goes his crazy imagination again. Still, he couldn't help fearing that the glowing orange figure, that fiery number three floating and shimmering in midair, was a dire warning.

Late that night, Lewis woke up suddenly. He had heard something, a creak or a groan. He turned on his side and looked at the luminous green hands of his Westclox alarm clock: 11:32. Then he heard something else: the front door downstairs closing with a clack. It wasn't a loud sound, because whoever had closed the door had done so carefully, but in the stillness of night it was about as noticeable as a firecracker going off beneath Lewis's bed.

Curious, Lewis threw back the sheets, got up, and walked barefoot down the hall past the bathroom. He knocked on his uncle's bedroom door, but he got no response. Lewis opened the door and peered into the darkness. "Uncle Jonathan?"

When no answer came, he turned on the light. His uncle's bed had not yet been slept in, though it looked as if someone had been lying on the red and green plaid covers. A book lay open next to the pillow. Lewis went over and glanced at it. He felt his blood turn cold.

He picked up the thin but oversized volume and saw that each page had either one big black-and-white photograph or several smaller ones on it, something like a magazine. The page that Lewis stared at had one photo that showed three men, each of them wearing a monk-like hooded robe. The picture had the blurry quality that some old-fashioned photos have, though the men's features were pretty clear. They all stared solemnly at the camera. Somehow, the shot looked like a very old one.

Beneath the picture, the caption read: "Three members of the Order of the Golden Circle, Edinburgh, ca. 1888. This very active occult society investigated magic, pursued its control, and researched enchantments. Members strictly adhered to the Rule of Three, forming teams of three members each for their investigations. Among its membership it included such luminaries as William, Lord Litton; accomplished barrister Sir Michael Moreland; and the poet and essayist Aubrey St. John, who reportedly went permanently and irremediably mad at the age of twenty-nine as a result of his studies of forbidden lore."

The Rule of Three.

There it was again. Lewis left his uncle's room, turning out the light on the way, and padded downstairs in his bare feet, turning on lights all the way through the first floor. "Uncle Jonathan?"

He strongly suspected, though, that his uncle had gone out somewhere. He had heard the creak of the stair and the closing of the door. Lewis opened the front door, stepped out onto the porch and into the warm, dark night, and looked off to the side. Mrs. Zimmermann's kitchen light glowed warmly yellow, and he caught a glimpse of her moving past the window. Lewis had been holding his breath. Now he let it out in a deep sigh of relief. He had no doubt that his uncle had gone over to consult with Mrs. Zimmermann.

And if that was so, everything would be all right. Lewis trusted both of them absolutely. Whatever strange thing was going on with floating, hooded characters in the shadows, with glowing orange letters, with the Rule of Three, they could take care of it.

Things couldn't get too bad.

Lewis went back to bed, and after half an hour or so, he heard the front door open and close again, and then the heavy tread of his uncle on the stair. The same loose stair creaked—it was the sixth one down from the top, and Uncle Jonathan was always planning to nail it firmly down "one day soon." A minute later, Lewis's bedroom door opened softly. Lying on his side in the bed, his eyes nearly shut, Lewis saw the familiar silhouette of his uncle outlined in the hall light. "Sleep tight," Uncle Jonathan said softly before shutting the door again.

Lewis relaxed. Some kids his age might resent having a parent or guardian check on them while they slept, but Lewis felt much more secure knowing that Uncle Jonathan had taken the time to glance in. He fell asleep not long after that and slept deeply and well.

The next couple of days passed uneventfully enough. By the time Friday rolled around, Lewis's black eyes had faded to a mottled purple and green color and the swelling was gone. Uncle Jonathan gave Lewis his weekly allowance of five dollars, in the big round silver dollars that Lewis loved because they were so heavy and solid they made him feel as though he had a ton of money. Lewis dutifully dropped one in his bank. He had started a savings account a couple of years before, and he saved a dollar a week. Whenever he had accumulated ten dollars, Uncle Jonathan would take him to the bank and he would deposit them to his growing fortune. He already had nearly $120.

"I think I'll go see a movie," said Lewis. "Want to go?"

"What's playing?" asked Uncle Jonathan.

Lewis got the newspaper to make sure, then said, "*Conquest of Space.*"

"I'll pass," his uncle said with a chuckle. "I can never understand all that science-fiction foofaraw. Why not see if Rose Rita wants to go with you?"

"I'll call her."

Rose Rita said she was bored and immediately agreed to see the movie with Lewis, Dutch treat. He walked over to her house and they went on down the hill into town. Rose Rita bought her ticket, and then Lewis reached into his pocket for his four silver dollars. He must have made a horrific face, because Rose Rita said, "Hey, what's the matter?"

Lewis pulled his pocket inside out. It had a frayed hole in it, and it was empty. "I lost my allowance!" he wailed.

"Hey, come on, it's not that bad. We'll backtrack and find it." Rose Rita tucked her ticket into her pocket, and they started back.

"Silver dollars?" asked Rose Rita.

"Yes," said Lewis. "Four of them."

"They should be easy to spot."

They walked along slowly, gazes glued to the ground. Lewis reasoned, "They must have fallen out when we were on the grass, because I would have heard them if they'd hit the pavement."

That narrowed things down to the lawns in front of Lewis's and Rose Rita's houses, the narrow strip of grass between the street and the sidewalk where Lewis had crossed first High Street and then Mansion, and the street corner at the end of Mansion Street. A couple of times Lewis was fooled, once by a smashed-flat bottle cap glinting in the sun and once by a discarded gum wrapper half-hidden in long grass.

But they didn't find even one of the missing silver dollars. Lewis trudged back into his house and looked in all the rooms he'd passed through. Uncle Jonathan saw him and asked what was up, and when Lewis explained, his uncle inspected his torn jeans pocket and clucked his tongue. "Sorry about that, Lewis! I guess it's time to retire those pants of yours to the rag bag. Well, I'll tell you what: So you won't miss your movie, I'll advance you two dollars on next week's allowance. Go put on some intact jeans so you won't lose these, and then go see your sci-fi adventure." Uncle Jonathan handed Lewis two dollar bills.

Lewis changed his jeans, and then he and Rose Rita jogged back down to the theater. They had missed the coming attractions and the newsreel, but they got there in time to see a Chilly Willy cartoon and the feature.

Lewis scrunched down deep in the theater seat and barely paid attention to the show. He kept thinking that losing his allowance was the second bad thing that had happened to him in just that week.

And he couldn't help wondering—what was coming next?

CHAPTER 5

A S THEY CAME OUT of the movie, Lewis saw Hal Everit walking along the sidewalk, just poking along with his hands in his pockets. Rose Rita called out his name. Hal looked back at them, hesitated, and then sheepishly came over. "Hi," he said tentatively. "Uh, I'm glad you didn't get hurt too bad, Lewis."

"I really got knocked for a loop," said Lewis flatly. "But I'm okay."

"I—look, I'm sorry that I ran away," muttered Hal. "I thought I'd killed you! I mean, I was pretending I was doing magic, and then you just fell off the bleachers! It—it scared me. I'm sorry."

"You didn't cause it," said Rose Rita. "It was an accident."

"We told you magic doesn't really work," Lewis reminded him. "If it did, I'd ask my uncle to cure these by magic!"

"Two black eyes, huh?" asked Hal. "I had a couple of black eyes once."

61

"What happened to you?" asked Rose Rita.

"I fell off a scaffold," replied Hal, and something in his tone seemed very odd, very cold, to Lewis. It was as if he blamed someone for his fall. "But I was okay. I had a couple of tricks up my sleeve that saved me."

Lewis jingled the fifty cents in his pocket. "Rose Rita and I were going to stop at the drugstore for a soda," he said.

Hal's face was expressionless for a second, and then he smiled. "I've got a little money. Mind if I tag along?"

"The more the merrier," said Rose Rita.

"Thanks. Really, Lewis, I'm glad you didn't get hurt worse. I felt like I'd called lightning down from the heavens to strike you!"

"Well, I don't blame you, and it wasn't as bad as lightning," conceded Lewis, hoping that Hal wouldn't continue to apologize over and over.

They went into Heemsoth's Rexall Drug Store and took seats at a round table. The chairs were made of fussy twisted steel rods painted white, with puffy red leather seats that whooshed when you sat on the cushions, and the table had a matching red Formica top. Lewis ordered a vanilla ice-cream soda, Rose Rita a chocolate malt, and Hal produced enough dimes from his pocket to buy himself a root beer float. "Did your accident scare your uncle?" asked Hal.

Lewis, sipping his soda through two straws, nodded. "Just a little," he said. "I think it upset him at first when Rose Rita called him and told him I'd been bopped on the head, but he saw it wasn't serious."

Hal nodded and then asked, "Hey, I've been wondering. Do you know how much those magic kits and stuff you were talking about might cost?"

Neither Lewis nor Rose Rita knew. But Lewis said, "You can check them out if you want—the museum is just down the street. But even if you don't have the money to buy a kit, there are lots of magic tricks that don't cost anything. You can get them out of books. Rose Rita and I learned how to do some for a talent show once. There's a cut and restored rope trick that's really easy. That's when you take a piece of rope, let someone use scissors to cut it in half, and then magically put the rope back together without out a knot."

"How do you do that?" asked Hal.

Rose Rita winked. "It's a trick," she said. "But Lewis is right. There are card tricks, and rubber band tricks, and mind-reading tricks, all for free."

"How do you do a mind-reading trick?"

Rose Rita gave Lewis a calculating smile. "You remember enough?" she asked.

Lewis chuckled. "I think so."

"Let's show him."

Lewis turned his back to them. "All right. Tell Hal to choose something."

Lewis heard Rose Rita whispering briefly to Hal. Then there was a pause, while Hal must have been pondering on what item to choose. Hal whispered his decision back to Rose Rita in a voice far too faint for Lewis to hear him. Finally, Rose Rita said, "Lewis, Hal is thinking of something special. It's here in the drugstore. Let's see if you can guess what it is. Don't miss!"

Lewis turned slowly back around. "Mm," he said, closing his eyes. "I must get in tune with the spirits!"

"Collect yourself. Ready now?" responded Rose Rita.

Lewis opened his eyes and glanced off to his left. "I'll bet he chose that great big red glass of strawberry pop," he said, pointing to a big fake iced drink on the wall above the soda counter.

"How'd you do that?" demanded Hal, his jaw hanging open.

Lewis laughed. "It's a code," he explained. "First Rose Rita told me the target was in the drugstore, so I listened close to her next sentence. When she said, 'Let's see if you can guess what it is,' her first word told me to look to my left, because 'let's' and 'left' start with the same two letters. If you'd chosen something on the other side, she would have said, 'Right, try to guess now.' If it had been in the center, she would have said, 'Send your thoughts out and guess.' Send, center, see? Then when she said

'Don't miss,' the second word told me to look in the middle. If she'd said 'Don't lose it,' the second word would have told me to look low, and 'Don't hide your guess' would mean to look high."

"Because *middle* and *miss* both start with *M-I*," Hal said, nodding.

Rose Rita chuckled. "Then I said 'Collect yourself. Ready now?' Lewis knew that 'collect' meant the color of the target was coming. And then I simply told him what it was, but you didn't notice. Collect, color, ready, red, you see? Lewis just looked to the left for something in the middle of the wall, colored red. The big glass of strawberry pop. Except it's not really glass, it's plastic, of course."

Hal blinked. "That is really pretty smart! You had me fooled, kids," he said.

Lewis shook his head modestly. "There isn't much to it when you know the secret and practice it. If you want to borrow a book on conjuring tricks, I have one that Rose Rita and I used when we did our talent-show act."

"That would be great," said Hal.

He walked back with them and Lewis went up to his room and found the book. Hal took it, shyly thanked Lewis, and set off down the street with the book open, reading as he walked. "I hope he doesn't wander out into traffic," said Rose Rita.

"He'll be okay," said Lewis.

Then came Saturday morning. Lewis woke up feeling better than he had since Monday. His headache was completely gone, his eyes looked better, and all in all, Lewis was ready to take Rose Rita up on some of her suggestions. Maybe they could ride their bikes around town, down to the waterworks and back, or maybe they could go for one of Rose Rita's hikes, exploring places they'd never really looked at closely. As he came out of his room, Lewis heard Mrs. Zimmermann's voice downstairs and smelled delicious aromas. That meant his breakfast was going to be more exciting than his usual bowl of Cheerios.

Lewis took the back stairs, which came out next to the kitchen, but somehow he stumbled on the third step from the bottom, flailed for his balance, and took a giant plunging step all the way to the floor. Pain shot through his leg, and he yelped.

"What in the world was that crash?" Mrs. Zimmermann appeared in the kitchen doorway, a spatula in her hand and a look of surprise on her face. "Lewis! Not again!"

Uncle Jonathan pushed past her. "Did you fall?"

Lewis sat at the bottom of the stair, clutching his left ankle and groaning. "I—ouch!—took a bad step!"

And so instead of having a tasty breakfast, Lewis wound up being driven to the emergency room in the hospital, where the nurses summoned Dr. Humphries as they prepared to X-ray his ankle. Lewis had to lie on a cold metal table first on his back, then on his right side, and then on his left side, while the nurses took the X-rays. Then he had to sit for about an hour while they were developed. Mrs. Zimmermann and Uncle Jonathan at least were there to keep him company.

At last Dr. Humphries came back into the room with the pictures. He hung them up on a light board. They looked like negatives, dark gray with the bones showing in misty white. The doctor said, "Well, Lewis, despite your best efforts, you did not fracture your ankle. You've got edema, which is our fancy medical term for swelling, and you won't be running any sprints for a few days. I'll wrap it in an elastic bandage. I think it would be better if you hobbled about with a crutch for a few days too, like Tiny Tim. Jonathan, keep ice on it over the weekend and if the swelling hasn't gone down a lot by Monday, bring Lewis to my office. Lewis, you stop trying to crack yourself up! But I think you'll be on the mend in a day or two."

Then they had to go to the drugstore to find a crutch short enough for Lewis to use, and what with one thing and another, they didn't get back to the house until after noon. Uncle Jonathan helped Lewis out of the garage, and they went to the back door of the house, which they had left standing wide open in their haste. In the kitchen, Lewis looked sadly at the big pan of congealed scrambled eggs on the stove and the cold muffins in their tin. "I'm sorry," he said.

"Nothing to be sorry about!" boomed Uncle Jonathan. "But you're going to have to be a little more careful, Lewis. It won't be much of a summer vacation for you if you go on getting bumped and banged around."

"It's all over now," said Lewis, settling into a chair.

Mrs. Zimmermann looked at him strangely. "What do you mean?"

"That was the third thing," explained Lewis. "The Curse of Three, remember? I got clocked by a foul ball, I lost my allowance, and now I've sprained my ankle. Bad things come in threes, and this is the last one."

Mrs. Zimmermann touched her chin with her forefinger. "Hmm. And just where, pray tell, did you learn of that particular meaning of the Rule of Three?" She glanced sharply at Uncle Jonathan.

He threw up his hands. "Don't glare at me like that, Haggy Face! I swear I never once mentioned anything about that silly superstition to Lewis!"

"No, I read it in an old book," said Lewis. "The book called it the Curse of Three. Rose Rita says it's just nonsense, but I've had a feeling something bad was going to happen."

Mrs. Zimmermann sniffed. "Lewis, I think Rose Rita is closer to being right than you are. Yes, there's an old folk belief that bad things come along in packages of three. However, bear this in mind: If a voodoo priest on the island of Haiti curses a man, that man will grow ill and die! Yes, he absolutely will. However, if the same voodoo priest curses the very same man, *but doesn't let his victim know he's cursed,* nothing happens! Do you see what that means?"

Lewis said slowly, "You mean that if someone just thinks three bad things in a row are going happen, he sort of makes them happen?"

Uncle Jonathan said, "Yes, or he makes too much out of small coincidental accidents that normally he'd just ignore. Yesterday you lost four silver dollars. Well, that's irritating, to be sure, and I know you miss the clinking of your weekly haul, but it was really no big deal, was it?"

Lewis shook his head. After all, he had been able to see the movie and enjoy a treat with Rose Rita and Hal. "But this really hurts!" he complained.

"I'm sure it does," said Mrs. Zimmermann. "And I'm truly sorry you injured yourself. But you were running down the stairs, weren't you?"

Lewis nodded sheepishly. "Because I smelled breakfast."

"Ah," said Uncle Jonathan. "It's your fault, Florence! You incited my nephew to an accident by felonious aroma! Speaking of which, let's get rid of these cold eggs and make us some breakfast, or lunch, or brunch, or lunfast, or something. I could eat a horse with the hooves and the saddle!"

"You're always hungry," said Mrs. Zimmermann, but she dumped the eggs, rolled up her purple sleeves, and went to work. In half an hour, they had an enormous egg and ham omelet to split, along with the warmed-over muffins (which were not bad at all) and some hash-browned potatoes. Lewis was as hungry as his uncle, and the two of them ate eagerly.

Mrs. Zimmermann had her usual small portion and sat sipping her coffee while the other two finished off the feast. "All right," she said. "As you know, I very rarely do things like this, because you don't squander good magic on trivial tasks, but after today's excitement, I am certainly in no mood to wash dishes. So—" She reached behind her chair and produced her old umbrella, which had a handle in the shape of a gryphon's talon gripping a small crystal ball. She stood back, aimed the umbrella at the table, and spoke a quick rhyme in some musical language that might have been Welsh.

Lewis pushed back from the table as all the dishes rose into the air in a swirl, then sailed over to the sink and washed themselves. A towel flew up over the sink, and as each cup, glass, or plate rinsed itself and went tumbling through the air, the towel caught it and dried it. Then everything found its own place in the cupboards, clinking and tinkling. It was all over in less than a minute.

"There," said Mrs. Zimmermann, tucking an errant strand of hair back into its place. "I think that covers everything."

"Mrs. Zimmermann?" asked Lewis in a small voice. "Yes?"

"When is the Curse of Three not nonsense?"

"Oh, my stars." Mrs. Zimmermann gazed at him. "Well, if I didn't tell you, you'd just poke around in Brush Mush's books until you scared yourself silly. Very well, Lewis. When a wizard or a maga wishes to cause ongoing harm to a victim, they often cast an evil spell so that it operates according to the Curse of Three. However, the three calamities that happen to the victim aren't just random accidents, like being hit by a ball or tripping on the stair. Somehow the evil magician has to tip off the victim first, just as the voodoo priest has to let his victim know that he has been cursed. And when someone really believes that one accident is a sign of worse to come, why, then the things that happen do seem to grow worse."

"Like being hit with a ball, then being accidentally shot, and then falling down the stairs and dying?" asked Lewis.

Uncle Jonathan looked astonished. "Good heavens, Lewis! Where did you get such an outlandish idea? You're not going to die because you fell down the stairs, and you're certainly not going to be shot!"

"No, not me." Lewis told them about the book he

had read and about Captain Lewis Nevins's unfortunate experiences.

"Hmm," murmured Mrs. Zimmermann. "You say the British captain was fighting in Spain during the Napoleonic Wars? Well, there were sorcerers at work in Spain back during the 1800s. In Spanish, the witches are *brujas* and the wizards are called *hechiceros,* and I suppose it is possible that one or the other of them cast an evil spell on this Captain Nevins. If he had been told that had happened, I can see why he would insist to his friends that he was bound to suffer three terrible accidents. But there's no proof of that. The captain might just have been a superstitious man. Lots of people are. Once they think three bad things will happen to them, they simply keep count until they can say three bad things have happened to them!"

"Maybe," said Lewis, and he turned to face his uncle. "But here's something else. The book didn't have anything about the Golden Circle. I know you looked it up in another one of your books, though. You started to tell me about it, but you never finished."

Uncle Jonathan looked embarrassed. "Well, there's not much left to tell. It's just that the Golden Circle crew enjoyed dressing up in those maroon monks' robes and drawing magic circles and dancing around them in the light of the moon, that's all. And their clubs were set up so that in each one there were always nine members. Three groups of three."

"So they could keep an eye on each other," explained Mrs. Zimmermann. "You'd have a master and two apprentices in each group."

"And you said your magic teacher had been a member of the order," said Lewis.

Uncle Jonathan sighed and glanced at Mrs. Zimmermann. "It isn't exactly a thrilling wonder story, Lewis. Back in college, I spent every Tuesday and Thursday night with a master magician who just happened to be on the faculty."

"Indeed!" said Mrs. Zimmermann tartly. "You know, I had no idea that the Michigan Agricultural College had sorcerers on the staff!"

Uncle Jonathan stuck his tongue out at her. "They didn't," he said to Lewis, "as Witchy Poo here knows very well. My teacher was a math professor by calling. But he also dabbled in magic and numerology, and over the four years of my college life he taught me what I know. He had learned his magic thirty years earlier as a member of the Golden Circle, and, well, teachers teach the way they were taught. Don't worry about the Order of the Golden Circle, because they don't exist anymore. They were pretty hot stuff in Great Britain in the 1800s, and they even had a group or two—"

"Or three," said Mrs. Zimmermann.

"Yes, or *three*," said Uncle Jonathan sarcastically, "operating in the good old U.S. of A. But, oh, right around twenty years or so ago, they had a big blowup, with members accusing other members of all sorts of shenanigans. Like most magical groups, they were a mixed bunch. Some of them were good people, some were just curious about magic, and some of them had the evil desire to use magic to gain riches and power. The good went after the bad, the bad went after the good, the just-curious ones dropped out, and when the dust had settled, not one of them could stand any of the others, and the organization just fell apart, that's all. What interested me about them really was just that they wore those goofy robes when they were doing their magical stuff."

"Quite a few of the people are still around, of course," said Mrs. Zimmermann. "But most of them are elderly and settled now, and I'm pretty sure that very few of them actively practice magic. The big quarrel that broke up their society seems to have made most of them allergic to anything sorcerous."

"Thank heaven for that," said Uncle Jonathan. "Some of them were really beyond the pale." He patted Lewis's shoulder. "Well, as it happens, you can rest easy now. I still say it's all coincidence, but even if it's not, you're off the hook. Your head got bonked, your allowance got lost, and your ankle got a nasty twist. That's three! From here on in, it's all smooth sailing."

Lewis nodded, hoping his uncle was right. But, as it soon turned out, the worst was yet to come.

CHAPTER 6

B Y WEDNESDAY, LEWIS WAS used to hob-
bling around with his crutch. His bandaged
ankle still felt weak, and he couldn't put much weight
on it, but he could at least get up and down the stairs
if he took them slowly. After dinner, Uncle Jonathan
washed and dried the dishes and then said, "Well,
Lewis, are you willing to stay by yourself for a couple
of hours? If not, I'll be glad to pass up the meeting
tonight."

Lewis realized his uncle was talking about the
monthly meeting of the Capharnaum County Magicians Society, a little get-together where generally
the couple of dozen practicing magicians in the area
just swapped gossip, nibbled hors d'oeuvres, and
played pinochle or bridge. "I'll be fine," he said.
"How long will you be gone?"

Uncle Jonathan looked at the clock over the
refrigerator. "It's not quite seven now, and I don't
think we have any pressing business to consider at

the meeting. I should be back no later than nine thirty. Are you sure you'll be okay?"

Lewis nodded. "I've got the number of the G.A.R. Hall," he said. The Grand Army of the Republic Hall, dedicated to New Zebedee's citizens who had served as soldiers on the Union side during the Civil War, was at the east end of Main Street, not really very far from their house. "I'll call if I need you."

"Fine," said his uncle. He bustled out, while Lewis hobbled to the parlor and turned on the TV, a nifty Zenith Stratocaster model that had a black-and-white picture tube with a perfectly round window, like a porthole. A Detroit Tigers baseball game was on, and he settled down to watch it, stretching the cord of the phone from the hall so he could call Rose Rita. Though she had become a White Sox fan, like Mrs. Zimmermann, she also liked the Tigers and would be sure to be watching the game with her dad. Lewis was just dialing her number when his uncle called, "Lewis! Have you moved my cane?"

Lewis got up from the sofa and without even bothering with his crutch hobbled to the front hall. Uncle Jonathan stood there scratching his red head. Beside the coat stand a tall blue Willoware vase stood, and from it protruded the handles of several tattered umbrellas and three canes. None of them, however, was the right cane, the one with a crystal sphere in the handle. That one was magical. That one was Uncle Jonathan's wand.

"I haven't touched it," said Lewis, feeling apprehensive. "Oh, gosh, Uncle Jonathan! What if someone broke in and stole it?"

"If someone did, it wouldn't be a bit of good to them," replied his uncle decisively. "A magician's wand is attuned to its owner alone, Lewis. No one else can use it worth a darn. The only reason anyone could possibly want to steal a magician's wand is that it would make the thief immune to the wand owner's spell, and—"

"What if an enemy stole your wand?"

"That didn't happen," replied Uncle Jonathan, "for the very simple reason that I don't have an enemy. Anyway, I could still punch him a good swift one right in the bread basket! But I don't know of anybody around who'd be nasty enough to cane-nap my wand. I simply can't remember what I did with it last. Oh, well, no matter. It will turn up, and the society doesn't have any plans to cast a spell tonight. Sorry I bothered you!"

And he went out, heading next door to ride down to the meeting with Mrs. Zimmermann in her purple Plymouth Cranbrook car. Lewis felt odd, his skin prickly. He stared at the mirror in the stand, but it just reflected his anxious face. He made his way back into the parlor. Wondering if maybe Uncle Jonathan had absentmindedly put the cane in the big closet where they stored their telescope, Lewis opened the door and flicked the light switch. Nothing happened—the closet bulb had burned out. In the dark closet the telescope loomed under its covering, an old sheet, looking like a still, silent ghost. Lewis took their astronomy flashlight from a shelf—it had a red lens, because red light does not interfere with night vision—but in its dim glow he saw no sign of the cane. Clutching the flashlight, he closed the door, got the phone, returned with it to the couch, and called Rose Rita.

"Hi," she said. "You watching the game? Tigers are ahead by two in the bottom of the fifth!"

"Listen," said Lewis urgently, and he told Rose Rita about the missing cane.

She was silent for a moment, but then she said, "He's mislaid it before, hasn't he?"

"Well, yes. Once he left it out in the backyard after we had a picnic, and once it was in the trunk of the car for a couple of weeks before he finally remembered where he'd put it."

"So he just forgot again."

"I guess," agreed Lewis unwillingly.

"How's the ankle?"

"Better. I'm still using the crutch, but I can get around pretty well without it."

"Your black eyes?"

Lewis made a face, though of course Rose Rita couldn't see it. "Yellow," he said. "Sort of a disgusting greeny yellowy, like those yucky little caterpillars that—"

He heard Rose Rita's dad saying something, and then she cut in: "I have to hang up, Lewis. Dad's expecting a call. See you!"

A second later he heard the click of the phone, and then silence. He hung up and stared at the TV without really noticing much about the ball game. He had not bothered to turn on the parlor light, and as evening came on, the room grew dark. Only the flickering gray light from the TV gave any illumination at all.

Until something caught the corner of Lewis's eye. A reddish light, not very bright, glimmered out in the front hall. Had he left the flashlight there? No, he saw that right where he'd left it, on the shelf above the TV, next to a ceramic souvenir in the shape of a baseball. A little terrified, Lewis got up, switched on the lamp beside the sofa, and limped out into the hallway. He immediately saw that the red light was flashing and flaring out of the mirror on the coat stand. Biting his lip, Lewis looked into the mirror. It showed a dark, flat land, with rings of tall, standing stones jutting up here and there, something like the pictures he had seen of Stonehenge in England.

But glowing balefully in the darkness was a gigantic numeral of fire, like the one he had seen the hooded figure draw once before.

Again, even larger than before, Lewis saw the blazing number floating and wavering in midair:

Lewis lurched back into the parlor, turned on the lights, grabbed the phone from where he had set it on the floor next to the couch, and frantically dialed the number of the G.A.R. Hall. He heard the phone on the other end ring three times, four times. "Come on, come *on*," he said between his teeth.

Then someone answered: "Hello?"

Lewis recognized the voice of kindly, vague Mrs. Jaeger, probably the very worst magician in the society. "Hi, this is Lewis Barnavelt, is my uncle there please?" he said in a rush.

"What? What? Lewis? I think Jonathan has already left. I'll check, dear. Just a moment!"

Lewis glanced back toward the hall, but the red light had faded to nothing. The front doorknob rattled, and he jumped a mile. A moment later, the door opened, and with relief, Lewis saw his uncle step in. At the same time, Mrs. Jaeger said, "I'm afraid you've missed him—"

"That's all right, he's here now. Thanks, Mrs. Jaeger!" Lewis hung up and said, "Uncle Jonathan! Look in the mirror!"

With a surprised expression, Jonathan turned to stare into the glass. "Do I have crumbs in my beard? Florence took one of her coffee cakes—"

"Is it still there?"

"My beard?"

"No, the number! Look in the mirror!"

Uncle Jonathan did so. "Nothing here but us Barnavelts at the moment. What did you see, Lewis?"

Breathlessly, Lewis explained about seeing the three. "I think it's a sign," he said. "I think it's saying the first bad thing has happened to you—you lost your cane! There must be two more to go!"

Uncle Jonathan shook his head. "I don't know. I'm going to call in Florence on this thing, just in case. I really think it's just this fool mirror playing its tricks again." Instead of using the phone, Uncle Jonathan stepped across to Mrs. Zimmermann's next door, and a few minutes later, they all three stood in the hall, looking at the now normal mirror.

"I wondered why you didn't have your cane," said Mrs. Zimmermann when she had heard the story. "All right, let me use my abilities to see if I can locate it for you. Come with me, you two!"

She led them to the kitchen, where she got a tall tumbler out of the cupboard. She filled this with water, then put one small drop of olive oil in. It floated gently, and at some whispered words from Mrs. Zimmermann, the drop of oil drifted to the exact center of the water's surface. "Lots of people think you need a fancy crystal or a scrying glass to pull off this stunt," said Mrs. Zimmermann quietly. "But the talent isn't in the crystal! A plain old glass of water will do just fine in a pinch."

"I thought magicians didn't use magic just any old time," said Lewis weakly.

"We do when we're looking for missing magical implements," returned Mrs. Zimmermann. She winked. "And sometimes when we're too lazy to wash up dishes, of course!" She stared into the glass of water for a few minutes and then said, "Now—show me where Jonathan Barnavelt's cane is at this moment, I conjure you!"

Lewis looked on curiously. He hardly ever got a chance to see Mrs. Zimmermann do magic, because she rarely did so. Most of the time, as she had once explained, her and Jonathan's job—and that of all the members of the magicians society, for that matter—was to prevent evil magic from occurring, not to practice good magic herself.

As Lewis stared at the glass, he began to see a faint glimmering glow in the water, a delicate violet color. It shot out thin beams here and there, and Mrs. Zimmermann's face, locked in concentration, showed flickers of the purple hues. She stared hard for five minutes, and then shook her head. "This is odd," she announced. "Jonathan, your cane is nowhere to be found! It isn't in the house, or anywhere in the yard, or as far as I can tell anywhere for fifty miles around in southern Michigan!"

"It can't have just vanished," said Uncle Jonathan.

"Why not?" snapped Mrs. Zimmermann testily. "It's a magic wand!"

"You know what I mean."

Mrs. Zimmermann nodded. "Yes, I do, and I'm sorry for sounding angry. I'm not, really—just puzzled. Your wand has a very strong morphic vibration. I should be able to pick up some faint signal anywhere within a hundred miles! Unless . . ." She did not finish the sentence.

But Uncle Jonathan did: "Unless someone is using some kind of evil magic to hide it from you?"

"Jonathan!" Mrs. Zimmermann twitched her head in Lewis's direction.

"Lewis is old enough to hear something like that," said Uncle Jonathan firmly. "And frankly I'm not sure now that he shouldn't hear a little more. Wait here, you two." He left them, and Lewis heard his steps on the stairway.

"What's he going to get?" asked Lewis.

Mrs. Zimmermann sighed and shrugged. "Who knows? Maybe a Captain Midnight Secret Decoder Ring. Maybe an enchanted pogo stick. With a big overgrown kid like Jonathan Barnavelt, there is simply no telling!"

A few minutes later, Jonathan clumped back downstairs and into the kitchen. He plopped a big, thick book down on the table with a dusty thump. Curiously Lewis peered at it: Its binding was black crinkly leather, with a golden rectangle stamped into it and beneath that a golden circle. The rectangle read THE WOLVERINE, and the circle showed small pictures that included an open text and a plow. Around the edges of the circle ran the words MICHIGAN AGRICULTURAL COLLEGE and the date 1882, the year the college was founded. "My old college yearbook from my senior year," said Uncle Jonathan. "Lord, more than twenty-five years ago! How time flies." He opened the *Wolverine* toward the back. The first thing that Lewis glimpsed was an advertisement for Gier Tuarc Steel Wheels, praising their beauty, utility, and economy. Uncle Jonathan flipped the pages, saying, "It's somewhere back in here. Ah, yes, here we are!" He pointed to a photograph of three figures, two standing and the one in the middle seated. They all wore graduation gowns, but instead of the flat mortarboard hat the other two wore, the seated man was wearing a fez shaped like an upside-down flower pot.

Lewis craned his neck. The man standing on the right looked familiar. Then Lewis realized he was looking at a face a lot like his memory of how his father, Charles Barnavelt, had looked in life. "Is this you?" he asked, pointing.

"I did not have a beard then," said Uncle Jonathan with dignity. "Yes, that is me, just prior to the Honors Convocation. The older gentleman in the middle, with the eccentric headgear and old-fashioned long side whiskers, is my mathematics professor and mentor in magic, Dr. Mundale Marville. And the crabby-looking fellow on the other side of him, who looks as if he had just swallowed a cactus and it went down the wrong way, is my fellow magic student, Adolfus Schlectesherz. He was German, come to America to learn all about growing wheat and potatoes."

"Funny name! And he certainly looks very unpleasant," said Mrs. Zimmermann.

Uncle Jonathan nodded. "That may be because, just two minutes before this picture was taken, Dr. Marville had informed Adolfus that he was not going to become a fully licensed and board-certified magician after all. He and I had completed our senior project—every pair of student magicians used to have to create an enchanted object, usually just some useless but magical doodad that contained equal parts of their magic powers to prove they were worthy of the rank of 'sorcerer.' Well, we had done that, but it was difficult because Adolfus was a pushy sort who never could control his bad temper, and since he had often warned Adolfus about that, Dr. Marville finally approved our project but refused to present him with a real magician's wand. So while I received my wand in a special little ceremony that Dr. Marville probably just made up on the spot, Adolfus had to settle for being named the Mathematics Student of the Year at the convocation."

Lewis stared at Adolfus. He looked older than Uncle Jonathan by five or ten years, and he certainly did not have a pleasant face. His narrow shoulders were bent forward, and his deep-set eyes stared out at the camera with a chilling expression of resentment. His prominent nose reminded Lewis of an eagle's beak, and he wore a bushy mustache and a dark pointed goatee that concealed his mouth and chin. Lewis shivered a little, just looking at this foreboding figure.

"Why show us this?" asked Mrs. Zimmermann.

With a sigh, Uncle Jonathan said, "Because as far as I can guess, there is only one person in the whole world who might resent the fact that I own a wand. I mean, the Izard family are all dead now, and I have no other magical enemies that I know of. But Mr. Schlectesherz really blew his stack when he found out I was to be wanded and he was to be turned away empty-handed."

"Where is he now?" asked Lewis.

"That's just it—I don't know," said Uncle Jonathan. "He went back home to Germany before World War II broke out, and I haven't heard from him since then. For all I know, he may have perished in the war, fighting for the Germans. But this is silly. Even if old Adolfus wanted to purloin my walking stick, it wouldn't do him a parcel of good. He couldn't use my magic!"

"Could he use *any*?" asked Mrs. Zimmermann.

"Oh, sure, he learned at least as much as I did," replied Uncle Jonathan. "A magician doesn't *have* to have a wand, as you know. A good wand is an enchanted staff that helps a magician focus and increase his power, but it isn't strictly necessary. And who knows, Adolfus may have found some other master magician to finish his education when he went back to the Continent. There were enough of them hanging around there back in the late thirties! That's where the big blowup among the Golden Circle really started, you know. If Adolfus hitched up with a couple of those, he might have become the third in a cozy little magical triangle."

"Oh," said Mrs. Zimmermann, putting her hand to her mouth in a startled gesture as she stared down at the photo.

Lewis looked harder. In the picture, the two students stood on either side of a desk. The teacher sat between them, behind the desk, his fez at a jaunty angle on his head. Beyond the desk was a blackboard with abstruse mathematical signs and figures crowded on it. And to the right of the blackboard, partly obscured by Mr. Schlectesherz's narrow left shoulder, stood a coat tree. And hanging on one of its hooks was a shapeless sort of garment that just might have been a hooded robe.

"Yes," said Uncle Jonathan wearily. "You've spotted it, Florence. As I say, Dr. Marville was at that time a member of the Golden Circle. But he was one of the good guys. And I might add, he never pressured either of us to join that odd outfit, and we never did. I never did, anyway. I just don't know about Adolfus."

"He may still have a mystical connection with you," warned Mrs. Zimmermann.

"Possibly, but I doubt it. When he didn't receive his wand, he lost his claim to be one of our group of three."

Mrs. Zimmermann began, "If Dr. Marville presented you with the wand—"

"He may have some notion of how I can find what's happened to it," finished Uncle Jonathan. "I'm way ahead of you, Haggy Face. In fact, I've been thinking about calling Dr. Marville for weeks, jut to see how he is. However, he is quite elderly, and it is now extremely late—close to ten twenty! So I'll ring him up tomorrow morning. I think he still lives in Lansing, though he's bound to be retired by now. In the meantime, Florence, you can do me a great big favor if you'd care to."

"What's that?"

Uncle Jonathan seemed to Lewis to be trying to put a loud, booming sense of laughter into his voice, as if he were proposing a wonderful joke. But his words were anything but funny: "Why, with your superior magical know-how and your personal super-duper wand to focus it, you can cast some protective spells over this house! Let me see. Linnaeus' Superior Ward, for one, and perhaps Alcazar's Charm Against Evil Enchantments. Oh, and Fogleburke's Sure-Fire All-Purpose Handy-Dandy Protective would be nice."

"And how about a nice fat red cherry on top?" asked Mrs. Zimmermann with an impish grin. "Yes, very well! I agree with you, there's no need to take chances, and I will humbly admit that my spell-casting abilities are better than yours, especially now that you don't have your cane. I'll run home and get my wand, supposing nothing has happened to it, and get right to work."

She did, bringing back her plain-looking old shabby umbrella. The only unusual thing about it was the bronze gryphon's talon gripping a sphere of clear crystal somewhat larger than a table tennis ball. Lewis knew, though, that it was a disguised version of her own magical wand. The crystal held great power and had been given to her by a powerful powwow magician, one who practiced spells of good fortune and healing in the Pennsylvania Dutch country. When Mrs. Zimmermann spoke a word of command, her umbrella transformed into a tall staff with a brilliant purple star at its head. Her ordinary purple dress became a billowing cloak with purple flames flashing and dancing in its folds. And she herself seemed to grow taller and fiercer.

Three times she chanted spells, and after each one the old house seemed to settle in a little more cozily, a little more comfortably. When the last spell had been spoken and Mrs. Zimmermann had returned to her everyday appearance, she brushed some wispy strands of hair from her face and said, "My heavens! That's the lot, I think, Jonathan. It would take a very powerful wizard indeed to break through those barriers—and if one tried, I'd know in a flash! Until the spells are lifted, absolutely no one can get into your house unless you or Lewis invite them in. I think you can sleep safe tonight."

"Thank you, Florence," said Uncle Jonathan. He started to say something else, looked hesitant, and stopped. Then he muttered, "One more thing. I don't really have any right to ask you this, but—well, we've been neighbors for a long time, and—and I don't know who else I could ask—"

Lewis's spine felt creepy. He thought, Uncle Jonathan is going to tell her to take care of me if he dies! His heart pounded, and he struggled for breath.

Mrs. Zimmermann touched his uncle's hand. "Jonathan," she said seriously, "you know you can ask me anything. We have been through the wars together, you and I! Ask away."

"Very well," said Uncle Jonathan, visibly steeling himself. "Then if you wouldn't mind—if it would be possible—if you could find it in your heart"—he took a deep breath—"how about bringing over whatever's left of that delicious coffee cake? I could really go for another slice or two!"

"Oh, you!" Mrs. Zimmermann shook her finger in Uncle Jonathan's face, but she was grinning. And she did go to get the coffee cake, and it was indeed every bit as delicious as Uncle Jonathan had said.

That night as he lay in bed, Lewis made himself recall the details of the robed figure he had seen in the mirror. It had a wand, a short stick, and it used the wand to sketch the number 3 in the air. However, it did *not* hold a cane—Uncle Jonathan's wand was much longer and heavier than the little one the figure wielded. Maybe the figure wasn't evil, after all, but some kind of mystical warning meant to protect the Barnavelts. That thought comforted Lewis a little.

And perhaps it was the cake or perhaps it was the protective magic that now enveloped the Barnavelt house, but that night Lewis fell asleep with no trouble and no pain from his injured ankle, and he passed the night in pleasant dreams.

The nightmare began soon after.

CHAPTER 7

ROSE RITA ANSWERED THE door and to her great surprise saw Lewis standing there on the Pottinger porch, his face pale and his lip trembling. "What's wrong?" she asked, letting him into the house. "Come on into the living room, we can talk in there. Dad's at work and Mom's out back with her roses." She led Lewis to the sitting room and noticed for the first time that he was carrying a thick reddish book. "What's that?"

"Something I wanted you to see," croaked Lewis in a voice very much unlike his own. He had marked a place in the book with a playing card, a three of diamonds from one of the many packs of cards Uncle Jonathan had lying around the house. "Read this."

Frowning, Rose Rita took the volume from him. It was the same collection of odd beliefs and super- stitions she had seen back on that first Monday of vacation, when Lewis had been sprawled in his lawn chair, munching crackers and reading. She saw that the chapter Lewis had marked was headed "Of the accouterments and paraphernalia of those supposed to be sorcerers."

Following Lewis's pointing finger, Rose Rita read:

A wizard's staff or a magician's wand (the two are often but not always interchangeable) is intimately bound up with its owner's life force. Although stage-conjurors typically wield white-tipped black wands some one foot to eighteen inches long, I have seen a variety of so-called "wands" in the possession of both men and women who fancy themselves workers of magic. These have ranged from a stout walking staff, more than six feet tall, belonging to an old man in County Cork, Ireland, to a curiously twisted twig not even three inches long that was always in the possession of an old crone of Glasgow.

But regardless of form or substance, all of the self-proclaimed wizards and witches told me the same thing: Whenever a worker of magic expires during a magical effort, his or her wand inexplicably snaps itself, breaking into two pieces. By this token, they say, they know the magician has actually passed away from the circles of this world and into the Great Beyond; for it is fully within the powers of many wizards and witches, they say, to feign death so perfectly that no one could say the wonder-worker had even a spark of life remaining. And so no witch or wizard is ever buried until his or her wand has been found to be broken in twain.

Rose Rita looked up. "So what, Lewis?"

"My gosh, Rose Rita, don't you see? I told you on the phone that Uncle Jonathan's wand is missing! This says that when a wizard dies, his wand breaks. What if it works the other way too? What if somebody breaks a wizard's wand? Do you think it would kill him?"

"No," said Rose Rita firmly. "And I remember a couple of years back, when a magician friend of Mrs. Zimmermann and your Uncle Jonathan died. They went down to his house in Florida, remember? And they had a memorial service for him and broke his wand then. So this isn't true. A wand doesn't automatically break when a wizard dies. It must happen only if the magician dies while using the wand."

"I'd forgotten," said Lewis as he appeared to relax a bit. He fished a handkerchief out of his pocket and mopped his face. "Phew! I came all the way over to show this to you because I was afraid to show it to Uncle Jonathan."

"You didn't use your crutch?" asked Rose Rita.

Lewis shook his head. "I stopped using it last weekend. My ankle's better, as long as I keep the stretchy bandage on it. And I didn't exactly run."

Rose Rita felt sorry for her friend. Lewis's face

looked as if he was worried half to death. She wasn't bothered by superstition herself—well, not much, anyway. She had a couple of lucky charms that she really didn't take seriously, and when she played ball, she always liked to wear her lucky socks and Detroit Tigers cap. But she'd never bothered about tossing spilled salt over her shoulder, as her dad did, to "hit the devil in the eye" and avert bad luck. And she never tried to avoid a black cat crossing her path, and more than once she'd walked under a ladder or had broken a mirror with no bad luck at all, let alone seven years of it.

"I'm surprised your uncle hasn't found that cane by now."

Lewis gulped a deep breath. "He's been searching for more than a week now. Mrs. Zimmermann says it's crazy, it's just as if it's vanished from the face of the earth. Uncle Jonathan thought he might ask someone about it, one of his old college teachers who is also a sorcerer, but he hasn't been able to get him on the phone."

"Hmm," said Rose Rita. "It seems to me *we* could figure this out if we put our minds to it. When was the last time you saw the cane?"

Lewis thought. "It must have been at the party, when he was using it to do his magic. But you were closer to him than I was, especially there at the end."

"With the purple smoke," agreed Rose Rita. She scowled thoughtfully. "I know he had the wand then.

Right after the show ended, he went inside to wash his hands before lunch. I don't remember seeing the cane around after that, so he must have taken it inside with him. I suppose you've checked the kitchen and the first-floor bathroom."

"About twenty times," responded Lewis with a hint of sarcasm. "Rose Rita, we practically turned the house inside out! And if Mrs. Zimmermann can't even find it by magic—"

Rose Rita nodded, nibbling her lower lip. "I know, I know, it must really be gone. Hmm. Okay, who's been to your house since the party?"

"Just you!" exclaimed Lewis.

"No, not just me. Mrs. Zimmermann's been there, and one day Hal came over to borrow a book. And there's the man who reads the gas meter, and the one who reads the electric meter, and the mailman, and—"

"Well, sure," said Lewis. "And the milkman, and so on. But I thought you meant, you know, anyone suspicious who actually came inside."

Rose Rita closed the book and tapped her fingers on it. Behind her round black-rimmed spectacles, her eyes were bright. "Watson, the game is afoot!" she said, quoting a famous line from a story about Sherlock Holmes, the great detective. "During the party, everyone was going in and out to use the bathroom and wash their hands and so on. I'll bet you anything one of the kids stole the wand!"

96

"And then what—took it to Timbuktu?" demanded Lewis. "Rose Rita, if that wand was anywhere within a hundred miles, Mrs. Zimmermann says she would've found it with her magic!"

"What," asked Rose Rita slowly, "if it was farther away than that? What if it was in Boston, with David?"

"That's crazy," objected Lewis. "You know David wouldn't steal my uncle's cane! He's scared silly of magic, after that deal with his house being haunted!"

Rose Rita had to agree. Their friend David was in some ways even more timid than Lewis. "But what if another kid took it and that kid and his family are somewhere on vacation, in Miami Beach or sunny California?"

"*His* family?"

"Or hers," said Rose Rita. "But there were only three other girls there, remember: Mildred Pietra, Diane Tieg, and Sandra Costick. The other nine guests were boys."

Lewis took a deep breath. Rose Rita was a great friend of Mrs. Zimmermann, and she always hated to hear him offer the least little criticism of her. "I guess it's possible. Mrs. Zimmermann admits that she might be fooled if the cane is a long way off," he said.

To his relief, Rose Rita just nodded. "Okay. So ten boys and four girls were at the party."

"Nine and three," said Lewis.

"I'm counting us," explained Rose Rita. "Fourteen in all. And if you want to count your uncle and Mrs. Zimmermann, there were sixteen."

"Yeah," said Lewis. "I invited Hal so there wouldn't be thirteen kids, I remember."

Rose Rita shook her head. "Don't start that nonsense about thirteen!"

"Well—the number three seems to have some sinister meaning!" Lewis exclaimed. "Why not thirteen?"

"Because if you start looking for it, you'll see thirteen everywhere! Your house is at 101 High Street. If you add those numbers together, one plus zero plus one, you get two, right? And if you add two to the last one in your address, you get 103! And if you disregard the zero because it's nothing, you get thirteen! Woooo!" She laughed a little at Lewis's stricken expression. "Oh, relax! It's just silly numerology, that's all. Look, my house is here at 39 Mansion Street. If you add those numbers together, you get twelve! But one and two are three, so if you replace the two with the three—oh, come on, Lewis! Keep your hair on your head, for Pete's sake. I'm talking nonsense, trying to show you there's nothing to this."

"Sorry," muttered Lewis.

"Where was I? Okay, I didn't take the cane, and you didn't take it, and I'm pretty sure you're right that David wouldn't dare even touch it, let alone take it. So that leaves us eleven suspects. I'll bet you anything we can solve this case!"

"But it might not have been anybody from the party," objected Lewis. "A burglar might have come in right in the middle of the night! Or what about when I got hit by the ball and Uncle Jonathan rushed over? The house was empty then, and empty again later when he took me to the hospital with my ankle."

"But why would a burglar sneak into your house and steal just the cane?" asked Rose Rita reasonably. "It was kind of battered and beat-up, anyway. I think if there were a cane-napper at work, he'd take a better-looking one, like that shiny black one with the gold head that your uncle sometimes uses when he wants to look snazzy."

"Okay," said Lewis, apparently giving up his objections. "So let's assume that one of the kids took the cane just as a prank, or because he wanted to pretend to be a magician. So what?"

Rose Rita reached for the phone. "So first we make sure Hal Everit didn't do it. What's his number?"

"I don't know."

Rose Rita called the operator, spoke briefly, and then hung up, frowning. "There's no listing for an Everit family," she said. "Maybe they don't have a phone. And I have no idea where he lives, do you?"

Lewis shook his head. "But I don't think he took the wand."

Rose Rita drummed her fingers. "I don't know. He pretended with that pencil, remember!"

"Yes," said Lewis, "but then when he thought he'd done some magic, he ran like a scared rabbit."

"I don't really think he's the thief either, to tell you the truth," confessed Rose Rita. "He lives somewhere in town, and Mrs. Zimmermann would have sensed the wand if it were that close. So let's question him, and if he's in the clear, we can get him to help us interrogate the other suspects! If we find that somebody's left town on vacation, or that somebody's parents mysteriously turned into Surinam toads, then that's our culprit. Are you with me?"

With a show of reluctance, at last Lewis agreed. But he didn't look happy about it.

As luck would have it, as Rose Rita and Lewis walked toward town, they met Hal Everit coming up the hill toward them. He gave them a sheepish smile. "Hi," he said. "I was just coming to ask how you were doing, Lewis. I heard about how you hurt your ankle, but it doesn't look too bad. You're not limping or anything."

"It's okay," said Lewis grudgingly. In a way, he would have liked to claim that his ankle was worse than it actually was. It was sort of fun to be the center of concerned attention. But he knew that Rose Rita wouldn't let him get away with that.

"Listen," broke in Rose Rita, "something very

serious happened at Lewis's house, and we think it took place on the day of the party. There's a sneak thief in New Zebedee!"

"A thief?" asked Hal, looking startled.

"Someone stole Jonathan Barnavelt's cane!" said Rose Rita, with the air of a TV detective.

"Gosh, was it expensive?" asked Hal.

Rose Rita jumped right in: "It was made from the heartwood of the Eastern Acacia tree, grown on the banks of the river Nile and harvested only once every century, under a waxing moon, by blind-folded workers who wear golden sandals. King Richard the Lionheart got a staff made of it during the Crusades, and later Robin Hood made it into his best bow—"

"Uh, no, it wasn't all that expensive." Lewis shook his head and shot Rose Rita a warning glance. "Not really, but it was special. Uh, he inherited it from my great-grandfather. It has sentimental value." Lewis was normally an honest kid, and lying did not come easily to him. Rose Rita wanted to be a famous fiction writer when she grew up, and she always enjoyed letting her imagination run wild. Right now, though, there was no reason to get Hal *too* interested in the cane.

"That's terrible," Hal was saying. "I like your uncle a lot, Lewis. He really made me think he was doing magic, you know, sorcery, instead of just tricks. Now that I've read your book about conjuring, though, I can see it's all simple trickery and—well, anyway, who do you think took it?"

"You didn't accidentally pick it up, did you?" asked Rose Rita sharply.

"Me?" Hal looked astonished. "No! I mean, you would've seen me, Lewis! Remember, you walked around to the front of the house with me when I was leaving?"

Lewis furrowed his brow. Now that Hal mentioned it, he did have a memory of opening the front gate for Hal. And he recalled Hal walking down High Street with his hands in his pockets. "That's right," he said. "I would've seen you."

"I'm sorry," said Rose Rita, "but we had to ask."

Hal shrugged. "One must rule out everything," he said. "No offense taken. But I don't know much about the kids at the party. Which of them do you think took it?"

"We don't know," said Rose Rita. "That's what we want to try to find out, and we need your help. It's a mystery, and we can solve it!"

"Like the Hardy Boys or Philip Marlowe or Sam Spade," put in Lewis.

Hal gave him a puzzled look, and Lewis realized that none of those names, all famous fictional detectives in books or on the radio and in the movies, rang a bell. "Uh, like Sherlock Holmes?" he said hopefully.

"Oh, right, I read one of those stories once," said

Hal. "It was about this man who sends a snake to kill his stepdaughter—"

"There's no snake involved here," said Rose Rita in a decisive voice. "Look, what we have to do is just routine, like they say in the TV show *Dragnet*. We have to go around and talk to all the kids who were at the party and find out if any of them saw anything. Or if any of them act suspicious."

"Oh," said Hal, still looking a bit confused.

"Look," said Lewis, "besides you, there are eight other guys who were guests at the party. Now, we don't think it was David Keller. So we have to talk to seven different guys and see if any of them know anything about the missing cane."

Hal listened to Lewis, nodding to show he understood, and in the end he couldn't offer any suggestions to improve their plan. They walked on into town, and Rose Rita set off to find the three girls and question them, leaving Hal and Lewis to make the round of the boys.

When Hal and Lewis climbed up the hill to Lewis's house, they came slowly, because Lewis was limping again. His ankle was a lot better, but the two of them had walked all over town that afternoon, and now it was tired out. Rose Rita sat on the front steps. "What did you find out?" she asked.

Lewis collapsed to sit beside her, and Hal remained standing on the front walk. "I found out that the kids live all over town," Lewis puffed. "I didn't think my ankle was going to hold out! Any luck?"

Rose Rita hadn't had any success at all. "Two of mine are out of town," she explained. "Diane is off at a band camp in Ann Arbor, and Sandra's folks are touring the Rocky Mountains with her this summer. I talked to Diane's grandmother and to Sandra's next-door neighbor. And the third one was Mildred Pietra, and I remember seeing her get in her mom's car after the party—without a cane."

"Well," said Lewis, "two of ours were out of town too. Alan Fuller and his parents must be away on vacation, and Trip McConnell is up in the North Peninsula, spending some time with his grandparents."

"How about the others?"

Hal took up the tale: "No luck, Rose Rita. Nobody remembers seeing the cane after the magic show at all, and nobody acted suspicious. Most of the kids left in twos and threes at about the same time, and it would have been difficult in the extreme for any of them to hide something as big as a cane."

"So we're right back where we started," said Lewis.

Rose Rita disagreed. "No, we have something to go on. We've got four suspects who have disappeared," she said.

"Oh, come on!" said Lewis, irritated by his throbbing ankle and his long, fruitless afternoon.

"Nobody's *disappeared*. We know where everyone is, except for Alan, and I'll bet if we went back and asked the Fullers' neighbors where they are, somebody would know that too."

Hal said, "It's too bad we can't use magic. If we could, we might find a way to trace the thief. I'll bet Count Cagliostro could have done it. He was a whiz at finding hidden treasures!"

Rose Rita raised her eyebrows, but Lewis just shook his head. "Yes," he said pointedly. "It's a shame that magic doesn't really work."

Hal sighed. "Look, I'd better get on home. I'll check in with you if I think of any other way we could help find the cane. I like your uncle, Lewis, and I'd like to help if I can."

"Sure."

As soon as Hal was out of earshot, Rose Rita said, "I think we may very well find that one of those four kids has the wand, Lewis. And I'll tell you something else: The thief probably wasn't Diane. I mean, Ann Arbor isn't that far away. Mrs. Zimmermann should have picked up on the cane's mystic vibrations, at least a little bit, if that's where it was. So that leaves Sandra, Alan, and Trip. Come on, let's go."

Groaning, Lewis followed her across the lawn and up to Mrs. Zimmermann's door. Mrs. Zimmermann let them inside, and they settled down at her table. Lewis liked her house, where most things, from the rugs on the floor to the oil paintings that

Mrs. Zimmermann had collected in France from a lot of famous artists, and even to the toilet paper in the bathrooms, were purple. Mrs. Zimmermann listened as Rose Rita told her about their deductions and their investigation.

"Heavenly days!" she exclaimed when Rose Rita had finished. "Well, I'll give you two top marks for energy, but as far as solving the mystery—well, no, you haven't done that, have you?"

"But," insisted Rose Rita, "if the cane were far enough away, Lewis says you might not be able to sense it, right?"

"Well, no," replied Mrs. Zimmermann slowly. "Perhaps not. But somehow it feels to me as if the cane isn't just *missing*, but magically *concealed*. Now, I can't explain it. It's a magicky, witchy sort of feeling. It's like—oh, it's like even if the cane is beyond my range, I should still be able to see the *shape* of the cane in my mind. Imagine a jigsaw puzzle with one cane-shaped piece missing! That's sort of the feeling I have, except the jigsaw piece hasn't even left a blank space behind it after vanishing. Still, I have to confess that it's just possible the cane is simply somewhere beyond my radar, hundreds or even thousands of miles away. But why on earth would a guest at your party have taken it?"

"Because Uncle Jonathan was waving it around at the party," said Lewis wearily. "Hal thought the cane might even be a magic wand. He said something about that just before that baseball hit me. And if he thought so, maybe someone else did too."

"Possibly," agreed Mrs. Zimmermann. "I have to admit I am getting worried. Something is going on that I can't quite grasp, and that always puts me on pins and needles. Well, be that as it may, I have dinner in the oven. It's my famous flaky-crust chicken pot pie, so if you will call and ask your folks' permission, Rose Rita, and then you will call your uncle over, Lewis, we shall further consult over a nice hot meal."

Lewis's mouth watered at the invitation, and the pie was just as tasty as he remembered, beautiful white chunks of chicken floating in a golden sauce with peas, carrots, and tasty little dumplings about the size of marbles.

As they all ate, Uncle Jonathan heard the story too, and he shrugged off their failure. "I will just bet you," he said, "that I've done something boneheaded with the cane and I'll find it sooner or later. As the old guys at the barber shop say, my remembery isn't what it used to be!"

"Does a wizard's wand really break itself when the wizard dies?" asked Rose Rita so suddenly that Lewis choked and had to gulp from his glass of milk.

"Yes," said Mrs. Zimmermann, "and no."

"What Prunella means," said Uncle Jonathan, "is that if a wizard is actually trying to use magic at the time of his demise, his wand will almost always snap itself—even if it's nowhere around him at the moment, even if he's not using the wand in his magic. But if a wizard just passes away of natural causes, no, it doesn't automatically break. That's why at a magician's funeral, his or her friends will break the wand ceremonially. That releases anything of the magician's spirit that is still clinging to the world and lets him or her go to a final reward."

"What if someone breaks a living magician's wand?" asked Rose Rita.

Lewis glared at her. He did not want to hear this.

But Mrs. Zimmermann, speaking with authority in her voice, said, "Well, there's a little more to it in that case. When a wizard passes on and the wand either breaks or is snapped, all the wizard's spells cease and their effects evaporate. I *think* that if a wizard's wand is broken accidentally while the wizard is still alive, it would immediately weaken the magician's power, just as mine once was weakened by a vengeful spirit. That could be recovered, in time, just like my own magic, which became strong again when I got my present wand. But if an enemy chose to break a magician's wand on purpose, after having spoken certain spells, then all the spells cast by that magician would freeze, would become permanent, and might even turn against the magician."

"But if they're just harmless illusion spells, nothing would happen," put in Uncle Jonathan hastily.

Mrs. Zimmermann looked at Lewis for a long

moment and then said softly, "I am not so sure. Jonathan, you said that Lewis deserves to know about this, so I'll tell the truth. Even in the case of illusion spells, well, I think the wizard might suffer something like a mental breakdown if his wand was maliciously snapped by an evil wizard. No one really knows much about that, though, and if *ifs* and *supposes* were posies of roses, we'd all have a colorful summer." She smiled sympathetically at Lewis. "Oh, I know you're worried, Lewis. But look on the bright side: Even though the wand is missing, it can't have been broken. Jonathan would certainly have sensed that—it would have pained him. And as for an enemy breaking it, well, Brush Mush doesn't seem to be any odder than usual to me."

"Thank you!" said Uncle Jonathan loudly.

Mrs. Zimmermann leaned forward, her eyes sparkling mischievously behind her spectacles. "Of course," she said, "even at his most normal, Jonathan Barnavelt is *quite* odd enough!"

Everyone laughed at her joke, but Lewis's heart wasn't in it. He kept darting nervous glances at his uncle, looking for any sign of a mental breakdown and wondering if that—a broken wand, and then a broken mind—might be the second and third bad things in a curse on Uncle Jonathan.

CHAPTER 8

DAYS PASSED, AND NO one could find any trace of the missing wand. At breakfast on the last Thursday morning in June, Uncle Jonathan said casually, "Lewis, would you mind spending the night over at Mrs. Zimmermann's house this evening? I have an out of town errand to do, and it may keep me away until sometime tomorrow."

"Out of town? Where are you going?" asked Lewis, his spoon with its load of cereal and milk poised halfway up from the bowl.

"I'm going to drive up to Lansing to see if I can find out what's happened to Dr. Marville," replied his uncle with an anxious smile. "I can't help worrying about my old friend, you see. I've had an uneasy feeling about him for weeks, and no one I've called seems to know where he is or what he's up to. Oh, he's probably just off on summer vacation, but I have to admit I'm concerned about his well-being. After all, he's nearly ninety, and I hate to think of him in his house all alone, maybe lying on the floor with a broken leg!"

Lewis didn't say anything, but he thought that he understood just where his own overactive imagination had come from.

Uncle Jonathan finished his cup of coffee and then in a voice that sounded a little too casual to Lewis, he added, "Anyway, I'm leaving for Lansing in a couple of hours or so, and I may not get back home until late tonight or perhaps even tomorrow afternoon. Now, I know you'd get nervous here in the house all by yourself, so Florence has kindly agreed to put you up in her guest room."

"Why can't I go with you?" asked Lewis. "My ankle is much better, and—"

"No. I simply don't want to have you out at all hours of the night," his uncle said firmly. "And I may need to do some snooping around in Lansing. I'm sorry, and I really don't mean to hurt your feelings, but I can do that sort of thing a lot better on my own."

"Then why can't I just stay here at home?" asked Lewis. "It's not like I need a babysitter or anything!"

His uncle grinned sympathetically. "Oh, you're old enough to spend one night here in the house alone, and I really don't think anything bad could possibly happen, especially not after Florence put those magical whammies of hers on the joint. Still, just for your peace of mind—and I'll admit it, for mine too!—I'd much rather you take advantage of Florence's hospitality, just for tonight."

"Okay," said Lewis with reluctance. He stared unhappily at his bowl of cereal. He had lost all of his appetite.

Lewis knew it was about a fifty-mile drive north to Lansing, the state capital of Michigan. His fifth-grade class had even taken a field trip there once, crowding for the ride onto a jolting, clanking yellow school bus that smelled a lot like vomit. It had seemed to take forever to get to the city, and then the class had toured the State Capitol building with its stretched-up cupola like an egg with the narrow end pointing straight up and its walls covered with nine acres of decorative paintings of everything from hibiscus flowers to worms.

Remembering his own visit, Lewis guessed it would take Uncle Jonathan about an hour and a half to drive there and the same amount of time to drive back. If he left at eleven in the morning and had good luck finding his old college professor, maybe he would be back by ten or eleven o'clock at night. Anyway, Lewis determined he would try to stay awake at least that long.

And so at about a quarter to eleven that morning, Uncle Jonathan put his small suitcase in the trunk, climbed into his boxy old Muggins Simoon, waved at Lewis, Rose Rita, and Mrs. Zimmermann, and then blatted off down the street in a cloud of bluish white exhaust smoke.

After a good lunch, Lewis and Rose Rita sat in Mrs.

Zimmermann's dining room and played cards with her, odd poker games like "Wild Widow," "Spit-in-the-Ocean," and "Pineapple." They kept score with toothpicks instead of the bag of old foreign coins that Uncle Jonathan always used. Unfortunately, Lewis's mind really wasn't on the games, and he couldn't always get the hang of the complicated rules, so Rose Rita cleaned him out pretty fast.

While Rose Rita and Mrs. Zimmermann fought a determined battle for the remaining pile of toothpicks, he went out to sit on the front steps and read—not the superstition book, because he thought he was already nervous enough, but instead a murder mystery novel by Agatha Christie. The story told about one of the adventures of a crafty Belgian detective named Hercule Poirot who lived in England and who followed a tangled line of clues to solve a puzzling murder. Unfortunately the tale didn't distract Lewis from his worries and concerns at all, because the very first time that Agatha Christie wrote about Poirot's "egg-shaped head," he thought of the State Capitol dome, and that reminded him of Lansing, and that reminded him of his uncle. Lewis found it hard to concentrate. He had been out for about an hour when he heard the phone ringing in the Barnavelt house.

Thinking it might be his uncle, Lewis hurried across the lawn, unlocked the door, and picked up the phone just as it rang for about the sixth time. "Hello?"

A man's voice said, "Hello? Is this Lewis?"

"Yes."

The voice harrumphed in a self-important way. "Well, this is Mayor Parker, Lewis. I need to speak to Jonathan, please."

Lewis's stomach fluttered. Mayor Parker! "Um, he's not available," Lewis said.

"Oh? Well, please tell him to call me as soon as he can on a confidential matter. I have to talk with him about some things I've heard," the voice said. "Thank you." And the line clicked.

Lewis dragged back over to Mrs. Zimmermann's house, his suspicions confirmed that the party was going to get Uncle Jonathan into big municipal trouble. Could legal problems with the city be part of the Curse of Three? Lewis thought about telling Mrs. Zimmermann—but the mayor had warned him it was confidential, which in Lewis's book was right up there with top secret. He sat on Mrs. Zimmermann's steps and steeped himself in worry.

Time dragged by that afternoon. After finally losing the last card game to Mrs. Zimmermann, Rose Rita came outside, and she and Lewis played a half-hearted game of catch until late afternoon, when Mrs. Zimmermann appeared in the back doorway to tell them that Rose Rita's mom needed her to come home. Rose Rita took her ball and fielder's glove, climbed onto her bike, and shoved off for home.

That was at four. For a couple of hours Lewis listened to the radio, paced the floor, and tried playing "Napoleon's March to Moscow," a fiendishly complicated type of solitaire that his uncle had taught to him, but he still could not concentrate. And though Mrs. Zimmermann cooked her famous savory pot roast, one of his very favorite dishes, Lewis had little appetite for dinner. To tell the truth, he felt relieved at nine o'clock when he could just go to bed.

The guest bedroom, tastefully decorated with creamy white wallpaper with a purple stripe design, had one tall window that looked out over the lawn toward the Barnavelt house next door. Through it, Lewis could not see the garage, which was on the far side of the house and behind it from his point of view, but he had a clear view of the front of the house and the driveway. If Uncle Jonathan drove in, or if he switched on the porch light or any other lights in the front of the house, Lewis would know he had safely returned.

Lewis lay on his right side, his right hand nestled beneath his cheek, and gazed out the window. The night was overcast and dark, and toward ten o'clock a thundershower rolled in from the west, bringing dashes of rain clattering against the windowpanes and flickers of lightning followed by light rumbles of thunder. New Zebedee could have some fearsome thunderstorms and even a tornado now and again, but this was mild by comparison.

The rain ended after about half an hour, and the

last reluctant grumbles of thunder faded off to the east. Lewis's eyes began to feel heavy and raw, as if fine, salty sand had blown in them, but still he watched, unable and unwilling to fall asleep.

Finally, just before midnight, he sat up in bed, exhaling in relief. The big, boxy antique car had just rolled majestically up High Street and had turned into the driveway at his house. With a satisfied sigh, Lewis settled back on his pillow. He felt tension flowing out of him, and at last he could relax.

Part of him wanted to get up and run home, but he hated for his uncle to know how anxious he had been. Telling himself that Uncle Jonathan was back safe and sound from Lansing, Lewis relaxed at last, and he was so tired that he drifted into a deep sleep within minutes.

The next morning Lewis thanked Mrs. Zimmermann for having hosted him. "I'm all ready to go back home," he finished, hefting the gym bag in which he had packed his extra clothes and his toothbrush.

"Is Jonathan back this morning?" asked Mrs. Zimmermann, peering at him over the tops of her spectacles.

"I saw him come back last night," said Lewis before he thought. He could have bitten his tongue, because Mrs. Zimmermann gave him a sharp, questioning glance.

Mrs. Zimmermann tilted her head, her expression

reproachful. "And exactly how late was that, young man?"

"Uh, I don't really know," replied Lewis evasively. "You know, we had a thunderstorm, and the thunder sort of woke me up." Or at least it had helped keep him awake. Lewis told himself it wasn't really a lie, or at least not much of one.

"All right," said Mrs. Zimmermann, letting him off the hook. She glanced at her gold watch. "Hmm. It's nearly eight. I'll go over with you and let you wake up Brush Mush, and then I'll prepare a good breakfast for the three of us. We can eat it while Jonathan fills us in about what he has learned."

The two walked over, crossing the silvery wet lawn and leaving dark trails behind them. After the rain the air smelled clean and fresh, and the morning breezes felt cool for the first day of July. Lewis found the front door locked—people in New Zebedee hardly ever locked their doors except when they were going to be away overnight—and he fished his key from his jeans pocket. He and Mrs. Zimmermann went in, and immediately Lewis pounded up the stairs. He tossed his gym bag into his room and then knocked on his uncle's bedroom door. "Hey, Uncle Jonathan! Wake up! Mrs. Zimmermann is downstairs!"

No answer came, and feeling a little sick, Lewis opened the door. His uncle's bed had not been slept in—scattered over it were pages from the newspaper, and when Lewis looked at one of the pages, it turned out to be the morning paper from the day before.

From downstairs, he heard Mrs. Zimmermann's urgent call: "Lewis! Please come here at once!"

He ran down to her. "Mrs. Zimmermann, Uncle Jonathan hasn't—"

"I know. Come on, let's see if the car is here." Mrs. Zimmermann walked fast down the hall to the back door.

They went outside and across the backyard to the garage. With a feeling of despair, Lewis saw that the garage door stood wide open—Uncle Jonathan never left it that way, because he was fussy about keeping the antique car protected from the weather. At least the black Muggins Simoon was parked inside. The car was empty, and Uncle Jonathan's keys still dangled from the ignition. Mrs. Zimmermann took them out and unlocked the trunk. Uncle Jonathan's small suitcase was still there.

"What happened?" asked Lewis, feeling panicky.

"I don't know yet," answered Mrs. Zimmermann grimly. "Close the garage door, please. And lock it."

Lewis reached up and pulled the garage door down with a clacking rattle. He found the right key on his uncle's key ring and locked the door. Then he followed Mrs. Zimmermann back inside the house. "Do you have a piece of chalk handy?" she asked.

"I think so." Lewis went to the kitchen and rummaged in the odds-and-ends drawer, sifting through bolts and nuts, can openers and coupons for canned soup that had expired in 1945, until at last he found a flat piece of gray tailor's chalk that Uncle Jonathan had used once or twice when he was making model sailing vessels and needed to mark some fabric for cutting out the sails.

"Thank you, Lewis," said Mrs. Zimmermann. She looked thoughtful for a long moment and then added, "Let's go into the study. I think that would be the best place."

In the study, they rolled up the carpet from the hardwood floor. "Now," said Mrs. Zimmermann, "stand in the doorway, Lewis, and do *not* come into the room, no matter what. I'm going to try something magical. It may look odd or even a little disturbing, but it is not dangerous. Trust me about this and promise me that you won't come in until everything is over."

"O-okay," said Lewis.

He stood there, holding on to the door frame with both hands, as he watched Mrs. Zimmermann lean way over, her left arm doubled to hold her baggy purple dress tight across her middle, and draw a circle on the floor of the study. She drew a concentric circle inside this, and then she began to mark the space in between the two circle rims with a dozen arcane figures, looking something like Egyptian hieroglyphs.

Standing up, she tossed the chalk onto Jonathan's desk and slapped her hands together as though dusting them. Then, absentmindedly tucking in a stray strand of gray hair, she turned slowly in place, intently studying the magic figure she had drawn. "Very well," she said. "Now, remember your promise. Stay just where you are, Lewis, and nothing bad will happen."

Then, walking slowly around the edge of the inner circle in a counterclockwise direction, Mrs. Zimmermann began to chant in a low voice. The language was strange to Lewis, but it held a great many growls, trills, and low guttural sounds. After making three circuits, Mrs. Zimmermann stood in the exact center of the two circles and held her hands out to either side of her, elbows bent and palms up.

The hairs on Lewis's neck began to prickle. A milky, shimmering light, like some kind of drifting vapor, filled the circle, and slightly denser, though wispy, white forms swirled all around Mrs. Zimmermann, things that almost but not quite looked like human shapes floating as though in water. They formed, dissolved, and re-formed. The perspective seemed disturbingly off: When the drifting figures were on the side toward Lewis, they were fully human-sized, but as they whirled slowly around to the far side, they diminished as if they were fifty feet away instead of only about twelve. The gray strands of Mrs. Zimmermann's hair began to stir and lift, as if a lazy whirlwind were blowing all around her. Every once in a while her head would jerk, as if she had felt a sudden electric shock. Though her lips moved and Lewis heard a vague, low humming sound, he could not make out her words. She seemed to be talking to the drifting wisps of fog.

Then, in something like a silent explosion, bright purple light erupted from the circle, so intense that Lewis squinched up his eyes. Mrs. Zimmermann vanished entirely in the glare. A moment later it had faded, leaving blobby dark patches wavering and dancing in Lewis's vision, and gasping, Mrs. Zimmermann staggered out of the circle and made her way to the armchair, where she collapsed. "My stars! I haven't done the evocation spell in nearly thirty years. I'd forgotten how much it takes out of a body. Lewis, be a dear and bring me a glass of water, please. And bring back a damp cloth to get rid of these circles. We don't need them any longer."

Lewis hurried to do as she had asked, feeling a weird sense of abandonment. The house felt *empty*, as if it had stood vacant for twenty years. Unremembered echoes lurked in the hall, unfamiliar shadows reigned in corners. His hands trembled as he filled the glass, then found a cleaning cloth and wet it.

"Thank you," said Mrs. Zimmermann, taking the glass from him and drinking deeply. "Ahh! That's better. Lewis, just erase those circles. Don't worry—

they're perfectly harmless now. Later, after the floor is good and dry, we'll unroll the rug again."

Lewis got on his hands and knees and rubbed out the chalk marks. "What did you do?" he asked, standing up again.

Mrs. Zimmermann finished her glass of water. "Something that should not be done often or lightly. I consulted the spirits regarding this house."

"The s-spirits?" squeaked Lewis.

"Not the wicked Izards," said Mrs. Zimmermann with a reassuring smile. "And your house is not haunted, Lewis, so don't worry about that! No, I sought out the spirits of good people who over the years have had to do with this house and then have passed on—there was a friendly carpenter who helped build it, a kindly doctor who had treated even the Izards, unpleasant though they were, and one or two others. I had to ask them, you see, because they were the only ones who might know."

Lewis dreaded the question he had to ask: "Did you ask them what happened to Uncle Jonathan?"

"Not exactly. They probably could not or would not have told me that, for the living can learn only a few specific things from the dead. There are extremely strict and clear rules about what I did, and while some evil magicians may attempt to break them, I am not about to risk that. No, I have a strange feeling here this morning, and I wanted to make sure I was correct."

"I feel it too," said Lewis impulsively. "It's like no one has lived here for years!"

Mrs. Zimmermann looked at him, her eyes thoughtful as she adjusted her spectacles. "It's even worse than that, I'm afraid. Lewis, you are going to have to be brave."

Lewis's heart quailed. He was bad at being brave, oddly not when he was in actual danger—he had stood up to terrifying threats before—but whenever he had to anticipate something happening, he quickly became a quivering bowl of Jell-O. Now it felt as if he could not catch his breath to reply. He only stared at Mrs. Zimmermann with wide, pleading eyes.

Turning her empty glass slowly in her hands, Mrs. Zimmermann said softly, "The puzzling truth is, Lewis, that all of your uncle's magic has absolutely vanished from this house. Nothing remains! It's gone like a candle flame blown out by the wind, leaving not a rack behind, as Shakespeare says in *The Tempest*."

"No!" Lewis said. He ran out into the front hall. The mirror in the coat stand looked dull and a little tarnished, and in it he saw only a hazy reflection of his own face. The mirror had never looked so woefully ordinary. Lewis tore to the back stair of the south wing. Here and there in the house were stained-glass windows, and that one was the easiest one to see from inside. It was the most vividly colorful of them all, and it always changed scenes from day to day.

But today it was just an ordinary leaded oval of clear pebbled glass showing no picture at all. Lewis swallowed hard, feeling a painful lump rising in his throat. He knew that his uncle's enchantments always tended to wear out if he didn't bother to renew them now and again. The strange, tiny figure of the Fuse Box Dwarf that had once lived in the cellar, coming out to shout "Dreeb! Dreeb!" when anyone went down the stair, had just dwindled away to nothing, and Jailbird, a neighbor's cat that Jonathan Barnavelt had once caused to become a whistling cat, had over time lost his musical ability.

But Jonathan had kept up a lot of the little everyday magic spells around the house, like the one on the stained-glass windows. If the enchantments were all truly gone—

Lewis rushed back to the study. "Is he dead?" he demanded in a shaky voice. "Tell me, Mrs. Zimmermann, I have to know—is my uncle Jonathan *dead*?"

With a look of pity and understanding, Mrs. Zimmermann replied, "I could simply lie to you, Lewis, but you are old enough to deserve the absolute truth, no matter how bad it is. And I'm very much afraid that the absolute truth is that I simply do not know."

Lewis felt numb. In a way, that was the worst answer she could have given him.

CHAPTER 9

*T*he first disaster could have been Uncle Jonathan's losing his cane. The second had been his disappearance. So—what was the third one to be? Death?

All day Friday Lewis fretted and agonized. Now he was sure his uncle was under the Curse of Three. He didn't want to think that his uncle had vanished for good—but what if he had? What would happen to Lewis?

He remembered all too well the terrible night when a policeman had come to his house in Wisconsin and had spoken with his babysitter. That was back when he was much younger. His babysitter, a high school girl named Gloria, had screamed, "No!" and had fainted. And then the policeman had told Lewis that a car had crossed the center line and had run head-on into the automobile that his father was driving. Everyone, his father and mother and the other driver, who had fallen asleep at the wheel, had been instantly killed.

Lewis had felt as though his heart had been ripped

out. He had only a hazy recollection of the funeral and the next few days, which he spent in a foster home. His aunt Mattie and aunt Helen came to visit him, arguing about his coming to live with them. Neither of them wanted him, and he had not wanted to go with either one, because he didn't like them. Especially his mean aunt Mattie, who made fun of him for being fat. She had once told him that he looked like a balloon ascension.

And then his uncle down in New Zebedee, Michigan, had agreed to take him in. Lewis had been only a toddler the last time he had seen his uncle Jonathan and didn't remember him at all, but he had rather go live with him than either of his aunts. Lewis remembered the long bus ride into Michigan and how desolate he had felt.

Now he felt the same exact way again. Aunt Mattie had since passed away herself, but he hated the very thought of going to live with Aunt Helen and Uncle Jimmy. Aunt Helen had all the personality of a leaky inner tube, and since she had become a staunch Baptist after marrying Uncle Jimmy, she moaned and groaned over her brother Jonathan and nephew Lewis because they were still Catholics. Short visits to their home in the town of Ossee Five Hills were bad enough. Lewis didn't think he could stand living with them, not every single day.

But Mrs. Zimmermann had at least a temporary solution. "If anyone asks," she said briskly once they had returned to her house, "we'll tell them that Jonathan is out of town for a while on business. That'll keep everyone quiet, because no one really knows what his business is!"

"He has stocks and things," said Lewis in a small voice.

Mrs. Zimmermann nodded. "Oh, of course I know," she said. "Yes, Jonathan inherited money from his grandfather, and he has invested carefully and has a tidy income from his stocks and bonds. But no one else in town, with the possible exception of Mr. Deitz at the bank or Mr. Conwell, Jonathan's lawyer, knows just how he earns his bread and butter. So our official position is that Jonathan is out taking care of some big business deal and that while he's gone, you're staying temporarily with me. That cover story will do, at least for a while."

"What are we going to do?"

Mrs. Zimmermann looked suddenly fierce. "We," she announced, "are going to get to the bottom of this mystery! We are going to find my friend and neighbor, and if he has been harmed in any way, those who did it will regret hurting him! Chin up, Lewis. As John Paul Jones once said, 'I have not yet begun to fight!' But," she added, "I am just about to start!"

Lewis called Rose Rita right away with the bad news, and she too tried to cheer him up: "If Mrs. Zimmermann's on the case, you don't have anything to worry about," she said. "I'll round up Hal, and we'll come over and see if there's any way we can help."

It took a while—Rose Rita complained that Hal's family didn't have a telephone, and she had no idea where he lived, but luckily, he had stopped by her house to ask about the search for the cane. They both looked serious at the news of Uncle Jonathan's disappearance, and a gloomy Lewis quickly filled them in. He left out all mention of magic, leading Hal to think that maybe an international gang of kidnappers had made off with his uncle, but clearly Rose Rita got the message. "What's Mrs. Zimmermann going to do?" she asked.

"She's got her own way of investigating, she says," Lewis answered carefully. "We agree that the first thing to do is to try to find out what Uncle Jonathan learned in Lansing about Dr. Marville, so she's gone up there for the day."

"Who?" asked Hal, sounding shocked.

"Dr. Marville," said Lewis, darting a sharp look at Hal, who looked very startled.

Hal gulped and stammered, "D-did your uncle have to go see a specialist or something? Is he really s-sick?"

"Not that kind of doctor," explained Rose Rita. "A doctor of philosophy, a college teacher that Lewis's uncle had classes with at Michigan Agricultural College."

"He must be old!" exclaimed Hal, his voice still oddly shaky.

"He's pretty old," said Lewis.

"Well, I hope your uncle finds him," said Hal. "Are you two hungry? Do you want to go to the drugstore for sandwiches and sodas?"

Lewis realized it was time for lunch. "We don't have to go into town," he told Hal. "Mrs. Zimmermann said I could help myself to anything in her pantry. She's got plenty of sandwich things."

They made sandwiches, munched them, and then spent a long couple of hours talking round and round Uncle Jonathan's disappearance. Hal thought that whoever stole the cane might have come back for Uncle Jonathan. Rose Rita confessed she didn't know what was going on, but she was itching to *do* something. The afternoon crawled by until four o'clock. They were sitting on the steps of Mrs. Zimmermann's house. In her absence, Lewis felt even more nervous than he had. "There might be a clue in your house," Hal suggested at long last.

"I don't think there is."

"But we could check," argued Rose Rita. "There might be something you've overlooked. I have to do something, I tell you! I can't stand just sitting around."

Lewis couldn't hold out against the two of them. They crossed the lawn, he unlocked the door, and he went inside. Hal and Rose Rita hovered on the porch until Lewis remembered that he had to specifi-cally invite them in because of Mrs. Zimmermann's spells. He hastily said, "Come in, come in!"

Hal grinned sheepishly as he and Rose Rita stepped over the threshold. "Thanks. I just felt kind of funny, for some reason," he apologized. Hal quietly closed the front door.

They searched the basement and through all the rooms on the first floor, though Lewis was convinced there was nothing to find. When he was sure Hal was nowhere close, Lewis even looked into the secret passage that led from the kitchen to the study, but it was empty and dusty. After two weary hours, he and Rose Rita ran out of places to pry into, and the two of them found Hal seated at Uncle Jonathan's desk in the study. He had a pile of books open all around him. "I've been reading," he said unnecessarily. "You know, we could *try* to use some magic. These books all seem to say that magic works, anyhow."

Lewis grimaced. He had not thought about Hal's discovering the books of magic in his uncle's collec-tion. "I don't think that's a good idea."

Rose Rita looked indecisive. "Even if magic is real, we don't have any training. It probably wouldn't work," she said.

Lewis's heart was thumping hard. He had never even told Rose Rita all the details, but the time he had tried casting a spell from one of these books, an evil ghost had risen from the dead and had almost ended the world with the help of a magical clock hidden in the walls of the Barnavelt house! "I don't think we should," he said, his voice thin with worry.

Hal held up a book. "We might have a chance. This book says that three is a very powerful magical number. There are three of us. It has a spell for finding lost things. Let's try it, just to do something."

"That's not a smart idea," Lewis said again.

"If it's just a seeking spell," Rose Rita said slowly, "I can't see the harm."

"But none of us are real magicians," objected Lewis desperately. "And anyway, I told you magic wasn't real."

Hal shrugged. "The book says magic is real. This is a simple spell that any student of magic can easily do. But if you don't want to find your uncle—"

"No, I do," said Lewis, beginning to feel trapped.

And so somehow or other, he found himself drawing another magical sign on the study floor, this time an equilateral triangle with one point to the east, one to the north, and one to the south. He finished, checked his Boy Scout compass to make sure it was properly oriented, and said, "Now what?"

"Now," said Hal, holding the big book at chest level, "I stand on the eastern point. Rose Rita, you stand on the southern one, and Lewis, you're on the north one. Just stand there quietly and think thoughts about Jonathan Barnavelt while I read this incantation."

With surprising fluency, Hal began to read a long, repetitive incantation in Latin. Lewis was good at Latin, but he didn't know all the words that Hal read aloud. He recognized many of them, even though Hal was reading at a furious pace: *invocatio*, a calling, an invocation; *sceptrum*, rules; and a sentence that sounded something like "I ask great powers for a turning back."

Lewis's heart pounded, but when Hal's voice grew silent, nothing seemed to have happened. "Is that it?" asked Rose Rita.

"That's all it says in the book," Hal told her. "Lewis, do you sense your uncle?"

Lewis shook his head. "I told you it wouldn't work."

Hal shrugged. "It was worth a try."

They obliterated the triangle and then replaced the throw rug. In the hallway, Rose Rita stared at the mirror so hard that Hal asked, "What are you looking for?"

"Thought I might have chalk dust on my nose," replied Rose Rita. "I'd better call my folks. I'll see if Mrs. Zimmermann is back and tell her what we're doing too, so she won't be upset if she sees lights in the house."

"We can search the two upstairs floors," said Hal.

"Okay," replied Lewis unwillingly. "But I don't think we'll find a thing."

Rose Rita walked over to Mrs. Zimmermann's house. The front door was unlocked, and Rose Rita went straight in, calling, "Hey, Mrs. Zimmermann?"

No one replied, and Rose Rita began to feel a little creeped out. When the phone suddenly rang, she jumped in surprise. But she picked up the receiver. "Hello," she said. "Zimmermann residence."

Mrs. Zimmermann's voice came over the wire: "Rose Rita? Is Lewis handy, please?"

"Uh, not right now," said Rose Rita. "Where are you?"

"I'm still up in Lansing," she said. "I've found someone who knows both Jonathan and Dr. Marville. And I've learned a thing or three from her! She's, well, of our kind, Rose Rita."

Rose Rita knew that Mrs. Zimmermann was telling her that her informant was a witch, or *maga*, as she preferred. She also understood that Mrs. Zimmermann didn't want to say too much over the phone. "What did you find out?"

"Get a piece of paper and a pencil," said Mrs. Zimmermann. "You have to tell Lewis all this as soon as possible. I'm leaving for home as soon as I get off the phone. What time is it? Half past six. I should be there no later than nine."

Rose Rita knew where Mrs. Zimmermann kept a notepad, the paper lined in light purple, and a pencil (also purple). She got these and said, "Shoot."

"Tell Lewis that his uncle's old schoolmate is indeed back in town. Furthermore, I think I know what—Mr. S. is looking for. That project that Jonathan mentioned is the key. I don't know what it is, but it's probably hidden in the house next door to mine. You know the one. It is vitally important that Lewis not let anyone get into the house. My you-know-what will keep anyone with evil on his mind from coming in under his own power, but if he's invited inside by someone who lives there, that's a different kettle of squid. Got that?"

". . . don't let anyone in," murmured Rose Rita. "Got it!"

"And let Lewis know that Mr. S. had a special study and was very good at it—the arts of confusion and concealment. He might be in some elaborate disguise. Of course, there are rules to ma—to the art, I mean, and the rules say he would have to play fair and at least give someone a chance at seeing through his surface appearance." Mrs. Zimmermann snorted. "Jonathan should never have had anything to do with that man! And Dr. Marville must have been pretty slow on the uptake not to realize that he was a bad lot! Why, just look at his name, for heaven's sake! It means 'Evil Heart' in German! Anyway, Rose Rita, warn Lewis. I'll be back as soon as Bessie can get me there."

"Okay," said Rose Rita, taking down what Mrs. Zimmermann had said about Dr. Marville and

Schlectesherz. Bessie was the name that Mrs. Zimmermann had given her purple car. She said that, viewed from the front, it had a face like a sleepy cow named Bessie that she had once known.

Mrs. Zimmermann hung up, and Rose Rita was just finishing her note when her hand froze. She had written: "Mrs. Z says Schlectesherz = evil heart in German."

She had spelled out "evil heart" on the page. Rose Rita was great at crossword puzzles and codes—that was why she still remembered the mind-reading code she and Lewis had once used in a magic act—and those nine letters tugged at her in an odd way. E, V, I, L, H, E, A, R, T. What was it? With her pencil she began to rearrange them. H-A-L E-V-E-R-I-T.

"Oh, my gosh!" She flew across the lawn to the Barnavelt house, reached for the doorknob, and tugged. The door seemed to be nailed shut. "Lewis!" she yelled at the top of her lungs. "Lewis, let me in!"

A bolt of sizzling green light leaped from the doorknob and struck her in the stomach. The next thing Rose Rita knew, she was tumbling through the air like a rag doll. And then the lawn slammed into her back, hard, and she lost her breath. Everything went black.

CHAPTER 10

"YOUR UNCLE SURE HAS a lot of stuff," grumbled Hal. He and Lewis had climbed up to the unused third floor of the Barnavelt house. They were poking around in one of the old bedrooms, which now held a million bits of junk jammed in willy-nilly. Lewis had just thought that if his uncle had been puttering around up there to look for anything, it would have been easy for him to lose his cane among all the clutter. "Does he have anything, you know, special? I mean besides his cane?"

Lewis shrugged that off. "I guess lots of this stuff must seem pretty special to him, or he would have dumped it. He inherited most of it from my great-grandfather, who used to have a great big mansion somewhere."

"Rich, was he, then?" asked Hal, and Lewis thought he heard a faint sneer in the question.

"I guess," said Lewis. "My great-grandfather Barnavelt made a lot of money with railroads and livestock sales and things like that. My uncle says he was a hard man to get along with, though. He and my grandfather, Uncle Jonathan's and my dad's father, I mean, had some kind of real falling-out. But then he liked the fact that Uncle Jonathan was studying in an agricultural school, because the old man had started out as a homesteader and a farmer himself, so when he died, to everyone's surprise, he left all of his money and possessions to Uncle Jonathan."

"It must have been nice for your uncle to have a fortune just drop in his lap."

Lewis was rummaging about in a closet, but the only things in it were stacks of shoe boxes that contained faded old photographs, the blacks and grays now sickly tones of brown. He felt odd, twitchy and nervous, and he thought Hal was sounding inexplicably sour. "Look, maybe this isn't such a hot idea," he said to Hal. "Maybe we should just go. Rose Rita should have been back by now."

"Let's look around at least." Hal rubbed his hands together. He took a yellow pencil from his pocket—Lewis remembered he'd had one that day when the baseball had knocked him silly—and began to twirl it in his fingers. "Does your uncle have any interesting mirrors?" he asked suddenly.

Lewis frowned at him. "Interesting mirrors?" he asked, his voice suddenly squeaky. "You mean like a shaving glass?"

"Because you see, my boy, I've been reading about magic mirrors," Hal said smoothly. "It would be about ten inches square, with beveled edges on the glass. And it might not always show you your face."

Lewis shook his head, now feeling something was definitely wrong. "That's sort of crazy talk," he said. "Come on, if we're going to look—"

"Where are the mirrors?" asked Hal. And all at once he—jerked. He shivered all over, his head rolling horribly back, his limbs loose. "Curse these spells!" he snarled. "And the puppet must hold the wand too!" His voice sounded completely different, strange, raspy, like an old man's voice, and oddly accented. A second later, Hal straightened up and smiled. "I really think we ought to look at mirrors," he said in his normal tone.

Lewis agreed—anything to get out of this cluttered, claustrophobic room!—hoping that once they were downstairs he could bolt for the front door. Something was wrong with Hal, badly wrong. They trooped from room to room as the evening outside grew darker. Hal snarled in frustration as he looked at round mirrors, big rectangular bathroom mirrors, hand mirrors, every kind of mirror but the right one. "It should be in a rich gold frame because it is precious and valuable!" he growled. "Perhaps it is hidden away! He'd never risk its being broken. Too much of his power is in it! Come!"

They made their way through the second floor, with Hal rifling through everything. Hal pulled pictures off the wall, peering behind them—a photo of Uncle Jonathan shoulder to shoulder with Lewis's

late father, Charlie Barnavelt, a rather good painting of the Eiffel Tower at sunset and a horrible one
of a knock-kneed brown and white spotted horse,
and others. Hal tossed them aside, and at least one
framed picture broke with a clink of glass. "Hey!"
Lewis objected, but Hal ignored him.

Lewis cried out again when Hal began to pull open
the drawers in his uncle's wardrobe, flinging things
left and right, and the boy whirled on him, his face a
mask of anger. "Be *still*!" he yelled, flicking the yellow pencil as if it were a wand.

And all at once Lewis couldn't move a muscle. He
felt himself fall sideways, toppling like a felled tree.
He collapsed against the bed, then slid from the bed
down to the carpet. His arms and legs had lost all
their feeling, and he lay there helpless, with the scary
sensation of total paralysis. He could see under the
bed. Hal was pacing around the room, muttering,
"Where is it, where is it?"

Finally, Hal stood over him and waved the wand
again. The old man's voice came out of the boy's
mouth: "I shall have to inspect in person! Come! You
must invite me in!"

Lewis rose to his feet. If he could have produced
even a squeak, he would have roared in fright. But
he couldn't. He felt as if he were a puppet. His arms
and legs would not respond to his will, but somehow
his legs marched him down the stair and to the back
door. "Open it," said Hal.

Lewis saw his hand reach out and open the door.

In the rectangle of night outside stood a fierce-faced man, skinny and tall. His beaked nose was the same as in the photo Lewis had seen of him, but his bushy mustache and triangular goatee had turned gray. He was clad in a faded monk's robe, with the hood down. He glared at Lewis from deep-set, angry-looking eyes. The man's lips moved, but the voice came from behind Lewis: "Invite me in!"

"C-come in," Lewis said, though he tried not to say it.

"Thank you," said the man sarcastically, stepping through the door. It slammed by itself, and he spoke a harsh, unintelligible word. Instantly vivid green sparks crept over the door. "We are sealed in," the man said. He grinned very unpleasantly. "You foolish children! You agreed to the spell that I performed through my puppet. You reversed the magic the witch cast on the house—reversed it so it now protects *me*, not you! Fools, so easily led. My wand!" He held his hand out, and Hal gave him the pencil.

The second that happened, something snapped, and Lewis felt that he was back in his body again, with proper control. "What did you do to him?" Lewis asked.

The man stared at him in evident amusement. "Do you think your little friend I have somehow enchanted?" he asked in his accented English. "That I perhaps have him in some way hypnotized? No!"

He laughed, an ugly sound like a rusty hinge. "What did I do to him? Why, you stupid fool, I *made* him!" He twitched the wand, and Hal staggered to his side in a dreadful loose-limbed shuffle, his head lolling loose on his neck.

"He is merely a puppet," the man explained. "Nothing more than a hollow shell filled with a little magic, to allow me to roam and spy, listening with his ears, looking through his eyes. And now I need him no longer, so—"

He pointed the wand at Hal, and zigzag streaks of green-white power struck out of Hal's body like miniature lightning bolts being attracted by the pencil eraser. Hal jittered and twitched and jerked.

And then he began to fall apart.

Lewis yelped in terror. Hal's left ear crumbled and flaked away, and his hair puffed into dust. His eyes shriveled, leaving two dark holes in his head. Cracks appeared all over his skin, and his flesh turned the sick gray-brown color of brittle oak leaves in autumn.

With a crackling sigh, the boy fell apart in a poof of dust that pattered down onto the hardwood floor. Hal was gone. Nothing was left of him but a settling pile of horribly crisp flakes.

"Now," said the man, "allow me to introduce myself. I am Adolfus Schlectesherz, and if you do not help me find what I must have, my fine young man, I will make you what Hal Everit now is! Dust!"

CHAPTER 11

"ROSE RITA! WHAT HAPPENED?"

Rose Rita groaned and opened her eyes. Everything was still dark—but then she realized that night had fallen. Mrs. Zimmermann was bending over her.

"I—he—they're in the house!" she wailed.

"Who?

"Lewis and that Mr. Whatzis, Schlectesherz! He's Hal Everit!"

"Come with me." Mrs. Zimmermann seized her wrist, and as if power were flowing into her, Rose Rita felt better. She got to her feet and ran to Mrs. Zimmermann's house. Inside, Mrs. Zimmermann picked up the phone. "First things first," she said firmly, dialing a number. A second later, she said into the receiver, "Hello, Mrs. Pottinger! This is Florence Zimmermann. Rose Rita was helping me with a few things today, and before we knew it, it was dark! Yes, time does fly. It's so late, I'd like to let Rose Rita spend the night here instead of sending her home. I just didn't want you to worry. No, no trouble at all. I have extra nightgowns and a new toothbrush she can use—yes, thank you! I'll send her back tomorrow!" She hung up.

Rose Rita had practically been dancing in impatience. "We've got to go! Now! He may be doing something terrible!"

"He may indeed," said Mrs. Zimmermann. "But we are not going to be of any help if we go rushing in without knowing what we're doing. Tell me everything, Rose Rita! Quickly!"

Rose Rita spilled it all, including the anagram she had made of Hal Everit's name. "You said he would have to play fair," she gasped.

Mrs. Zimmermann's expression was grim. "Yes, and that is just the kind of smart-aleck clue that a man like Schlectesherz would leave! But I don't see how he could manage to make himself young! That is very powerful magic indeed, and it should be far beyond someone who couldn't even earn a wand."

"What is he after?" asked Rose Rita.

"Only the senior project that he and Jonathan magically created together all those years ago. A magician's first magically-made artifact binds and locks his power. If it's something made by two people, then it holds magic from both of them. If one of them *unmakes* the artifact alone, then he or she becomes twice as powerful."

"Then—then Lewis's uncle might have been—" Rose Rita broke off with a sob.

"Murdered? Not by Schlectesherz. If one of the creators of a magical item is killed by the other, then that item not only loses all of its power, but it drains that of the murderer. And just breaking the item won't work either. No, before he disposed of Jonathan, old Droopy Drawers would first have to go through the complicated magical process of unmaking their project to gain all of Jonathan's power. That's what the evil-hearted Schlectesherz is after—power!"

"Lewis is in there with him, all alone! We have to help him!"

"So we do. Come on!"

Mrs. Zimmermann grabbed her umbrella, and she and Rose Rita marched back across the lawn. The Barnavelt house stood completely dark, but when Rose Rita looked closely, she saw an occasional small sliver of yellow light beneath a door here or beside a window sash there. Something was blocking the light that should have streamed from the windows. It looked as if some giant had poured India ink down the chimney of the house, filling every room to the top.

Mrs. Zimmermann murmured a spell and swept her wand through the air. Rose Rita bit her lip. Suddenly revealed, and creeping over every inch of the house, were what looked like snakes, glowing green misty vipers that writhed and crawled over and under one another.

"The Serpent Lock," growled Mrs. Zimmermann. "No wonder you got knocked off the porch! That's

144

a strong protective spell. I don't know how someone like Schlectesherz could have pulled it off."

"Maybe—maybe he used your magic," said Rose Rita, and she haltingly told about the spell Hal had persuaded her and Lewis to try.

"That's it," said Mrs. Zimmermann grimly. "He could never have broken through my magic from outside—but once inside its field of power, he could change and alter it, and that's just what he's done! He's turned my own magic against us! Step back. I'm going to try something."

Pointing her wand at the front door, she said something else. Rose Rita saw a purple beam of light stream out and strike the writhing mass of vaporous snakes where the front door should be. The creatures squirmed away from the surging beam, leaving a growing oval that soon revealed the whole door. "I thought there might be just enough of my own touch left in the spell to let me do that. Come on," said Mrs. Zimmermann. "We should be able to get in now. Don't touch the walls! And don't look into their horrible little red beady eyes!"

Breathing fast, Rose Rita followed her. Mrs. Zimmermann reached out gingerly, grasped the doorknob, and opened the door. "Inside, quick!"

They rushed through, and Mrs. Zimmermann quietly closed the door behind her. "Now," she whispered, "not a word until I get some sense of what is going on."

Just then Rose Rita heard muffled voices from somewhere toward the back of the house. She shot Mrs. Zimmermann an inquiring glance, but the witch shook her head and formed the word *wait* on her lips without actually making a sound.

Rose Rita balled her hands into fists. She couldn't stand much of this! She wanted to—to do something!

Mrs. Zimmermann grabbed her arm above the elbow and pulled her into the darkened parlor. She silently swung the door almost closed and stood so that both she and Rose Rita could look out. Into Rose Rita's ear she whispered, "Wait. Can't use my magic because he's changed it. Might kill us if I tried. Be quiet and wait."

Rose Rita felt sick. Lewis came stumbling in with a thin man close behind him, a man wearing a faded monk's robe. He held a wand in his hand, a thin, yellow, shimmering wand, and it was pointed at Lewis's back. "Where?" the man asked in a harsh voice.

A shuddering Lewis pointed toward the coat stand. "That?" growled the man. He flicked his wand and snapped, "Reveal!"

Green light shimmered on the coat stand for a moment, and then it faded away. "Nothing!" the man said. "Lie to me, will you?"

"No," gasped Lewis. "I swear! Up until Uncle Jonathan vanished, it showed p-pictures of strange lands and even alien p-planets! It's the only magic

146

mirror in the house that I know about, but now it's all tarnished and dark!"

The man stared at the mirror in a kind of baffled rage. "Potbelly Barnavelt couldn't be that good! That he would be smart enough to hide the invaluable mirror in plain sight, so that my puppet never took a close look at it, I might believe. But he can't have the power to disguise the mirror against my spell of revelation! I put something of myself into it too, you know!"

"I d-don't know," insisted poor Lewis, and the agony in his voice made Rose Rita's heart hurt. "He never told me how it was made!"

"I will disperse any of your uncle's magic that might linger on it. Then we will see."

"There isn't any magic!" wailed Lewis. "It's all gone!"

The man stared at him. Then he did an odd thing. With his free left hand, he began to sweep his fingers through the air, as though trying to catch invisible cobwebs. "Can it be? How can it be? I did not kill him! His wand is unbroken! Or is it?" With a furious jerk, he flung the front door open and hissed some strange words out into the darkness. "We shall know in a moment." He chuckled grimly. "The people in this stupid little town are such fools! Do you know that if the school had ever checked to find just where Hal Everit lived, the address would have been a tomb in the cemetery? Ah—here it comes!" He held out his hand, and with a solid smack something flew in through the doorway and into his palm.

He held it out before him. "No," he said. "Not broken."

Rose Rita heard Lewis gasp.

The thing that had sailed in from the night was his uncle's magic wand.

CHAPTER 12

"YOU WANT THIS?" ASKED Schlectesherz, teasing Lewis with the cane. He held it almost within reach, then sneeringly moved it away as Lewis tried to grab for it. "Take it!"

"You don't have any right to it!" said Lewis furiously. "It's Uncle Jonathan's!"

"Yes," derided the magician. "It is your uncle's, the great lump, the fool who thinks magic should be used to amuse snot-nosed children. And of course you have no magic yourself. You must truly be a great weakling. He's never taught you a thing!"

"I don't even want to learn to do magic!" Lewis said. "I'm—I'm—not—"

"You're not brave enough!" Schlectesherz closed the front door. "Not like me! I see what I want, and I take it. You will never have that kind of courage, never! You idiot, didn't you realize that my pet puppet Hal waved my wand and caused that ball to hit you? That got you and your uncle out of the way, but not long enough! I sent Hal into your house, then and again after he made you fall on the stair, and that time he took the wand so that Barnavelt could not against me act if he suspected anything, but the puppet could not find what I sought!"

"You're nothing but—but a rotten thief!" said Lewis, feeling his face glowing hot with anger and frustration. "You're no magician. You just steal what other people have!"

"You think so? You say this is your uncle's property?" The bearded man held the cane at the center and offered it to Lewis. "Very well. Here. Take this. Hold it. Your uncle will sense that, wherever he is. He will know that you have the wand—and that I have *you*! If he is somehow keeping a spell of concealment on this mirror, that will make him take it off!"

Lewis held the cane. It felt dead and heavy in his hands. He couldn't sense his uncle's presence at all, and as badly as he wished he could do magic at the moment, he had no idea of how he could even try to wield the wand. He fought back frightened, angry sobs.

Schlectesherz had backed cautiously away, his wand still leveled at Lewis's chest. "Jonathan Barnavelt!" the man shouted. "If you can hear me, you know what I can do to your nephew! I can make him blind and mindless! I can shut him up in a tomb with scuttling flesh-eating spiders and hungry worms! I can freeze him like a statue so that he will for a thousand thousand years live but will be unable to move or make a sound or even breathe in all that time! I've learned so much since our *master* humiliated me! When in my homeland a mob tried to hang me, I lived by virtue of my magic! I have even won my own wand!"

Lewis stood nervously grasping the cane almost as if it were a baseball bat. He thought he might take a swat at Schlectesherz—but the man was out of reach, and something told Lewis that if he made a false move, that yellow wand would freeze him again in a second. He thought furiously, *Uncle Jonathan, if you can hear me, don't do what he says! He won't do anything to me as long as he can't get what he wants!*

A long silence dragged on and on. "Tell him, boy," the man said menacingly, moving his wand in threatening little circles. "Tell him to take his protective enchantment off the mirror right now, or else I promise you, you will think an agonizing death a good alternative to what I plan to do to you!"

"Uncle Jonathan!" shouted Lewis. "Don't do it! He can't hurt me if he doesn't have the mirror!"

"You think not, eh? You foolish boy, I warned you!" Schlectesherz drew his arm back, his hand raised almost to shoulder height, pointing the wand—it seemed to flicker, now just a yellow pencil, now a long yellowish magical scepter—and at that moment the mirror in the coatrack suddenly began to flash scarlet, as though a silent thunderstorm raged in its depths.

"Ah!" shouted the magician, taking a step back. "You have made a wise choice, Jonathan Barnavelt!"

Rays of crimson light spiked out of the mirror, peppering the hallway walls with spots of bloody, glowing scarlet. The entire surface glittered with flashes of red. The light went out, came back, went out, and came back—three times!

"What?" roared Schlectesherz. "No, impossible! There is no three! There are only two! The old man I killed in a magic duel! You lie!"

And then from the parlor door something white streaked through the air. It smacked hard into the mirror and with a loud glassy *crack!* the mirror shattered, half of it falling out of the frame and tinkling as it fell. The white thing thudded to the floor, unbroken, and rolled to Lewis's feet. He recognized it at once. Someone had thrown the ceramic knickknack in the shape of a baseball with the words "Souvenir of Tiger Stadium" written on it in red script. Lewis remembered that it had been on a shelf above the TV set.

The parlor door opened all the way, and Mrs. Zimmermann stepped out. She grasped her tall wand with the purple star flaming at its tip, and she held it as if it were a lance, its business end pointed at the dumbfounded evil sorcerer. "That will be enough!" she said. "Adolfus Schlectesherz, I have broken your mirror and have taken your powers!"

"You interfering old witch! I'll show you my powers!" Schlectesherz raised his wand—

And with a crack, Lewis swept his uncle's cane in a slashing arc, swinging it as if it were an axe. He couldn't use it to do magic—but he could use it to break something as small as a pencil!

A silent explosion of green light flooded the hall. The evil magician shrieked, "No!" He lifted his wand, his mouth open in shock, and he stared at what he held: a broken-off yellow pencil, three or four inches of it missing.

The green light spurted from the broken end and immediately condensed like a fog, forming a swirling whirlpool in midair. At the center of it, a white oval of light appeared and swelled in an instant to an irregular, pulsing, six-foot-tall glimmer. A moment later, a familiar, rumpled figure came barrel-rolling out of it. Uncle Jonathan yelled, "My wand, Lewis!"

A cursing Schlectesherz threw down the stub of his wand and raised his hands, fingers crooked like talons, and snarled a magic spell. He was half a heartbeat too slow. Uncle Jonathan, clutching his own wand, spoke a quick charm and the snaky green bursts of light from the evil magician's fingers simply evaporated before they touched him. "You've lost your little wand," said Uncle Jonathan. "Its power to do more mischief has ended, but now all the spells you created with it are frozen in time and turning against you. You know what that means—you have to pay for all the evil your spells have caused. And to begin with, you have to be taken to the prison you created for me!"

"No," said Schlectesherz, wringing his hands together as though Uncle Jonathan's spell had made them ache. "I beat that imbecile Marville, and I'll beat you, if I have to batter you senseless with your own cane! Marville was always Number One in our group, you Number Two, and I Number Three, the least of them—but I shall be greatest! You pompous fat windbag, I'll—"

"You will what, Adolfus?"

Lewis gasped at the sound of the level, calm voice. Standing in front of the whirling pool of light was a man dressed in the flowing maroon robe of a member of the Golden Circle. He raised his long-fingered hands and lowered the hood that hid his face. It was the side-whiskered Dr. Marville, much as he had looked in the photo, except now his whole being seemed filled with a clear, strong light. "You did not defeat me, Number Three," the apparition said tranquilly. "You merely killed me, and that is not the same thing. Now come! I order you to follow me!" He stepped back into the pool of light, beckoning.

"No!" whined Schlectesherz, writhing and squirming, sweat dripping from his face. "No, you can't make me go!"

But it seemed he could. Leaning desperately backward, Schlectesherz resisted with all his might. The effort was useless. A horrified Lewis saw that his body, like that of Hal Everit, was *dissolving,* unraveling into roiling, whipping streamers of muddy gray smoke. They went swirling and twisting into the whirlpool of light, and the magician became less and less substantial, fading away to transparency. He screamed and twitched and shrieked, and suddenly even the sound was being pulled away, like the sound of a distant retreating train whistle late at night. The spiral of light lost its sickly green color, became clear and white, pulsed strongly, and then Schlectesherz simply wasn't *there* any longer.

The light blinked out.

Lewis stood trembling and gasping, not completely sure of what had just happened, or whether it was over yet.

"Everyone okay?" his uncle asked, running a hand through his rumpled red hair. "Florence, Rose Rita, glad you could make it. What day is it?"

"Friday," said Rose Rita. "July first."

"No," said Mrs. Zimmermann, raising her finger and tilting her head. "It's Saturday, July second. The witching hour has just struck."

And then Lewis heard it, from the study down the hall: The cranky old grandfather clock was striking midnight. It sounded horrible, like a trunk full of tin plates falling slowly and solemnly down a flight of stairs.

For the first year or so that he had lived with his uncle, Lewis had come to hate the clunky, clanky gonging of that old clock. It was a sound that woke him up sometimes at night, it was an unmusical, grating noise, it was—well, at that moment, it was the sweetest sound that Lewis had ever heard.

CHAPTER 13

Sunday passed quietly. Then the next morning, the Fourth of July dawned overcast, but as the day went on, a warm breeze from the west swept the gray clouds off toward Detroit and Toledo. Lewis couldn't get used to the fact that his uncle was back safe and sound. He still felt very wobbly on his legs, but he followed Uncle Jonathan around the house like a puppy, bursting with questions and getting no answers at all. But that afternoon Rose Rita came over, and so did Mrs. Zimmermann, and in the Barnavelt parlor they sat sorting out everything that had happened.

"Where did you go when Schlectesherz zapped you?" asked Rose Rita.

Uncle Jonathan made a face and tugged at his red beard. "I don't really know! Into the abomination of desolation, or the not-so-wonderful Land of Ooze, or some alternate dimension, I guess. It all seemed like a dream—one of those dreams you get when you're in the hospital after an operation and you're still fight-

157

ing off the anesthetic. What saved my sanity was that Dr. Marville was there too, or at least his spirit was. He spooked me at first because he appeared to be wearing that maroon robe that Lewis talked so much about, but that was the only way he could take form so I could see him."

"Wait, wait. Start at the beginning. How did old Evil Heart catch you out?" asked Mrs. Zimmermann.

"My fault," confessed Uncle Jonathan. "I'd spent a fruitless day in Lansing trying to hunt down Dr. Marville, or at least find someone who knew what had happened to him. I finally tracked down his housekeeper, who told me that at the end of April she had come in one morning and had found a typewritten note, supposedly from the doc, telling her that he had been called away on urgent family business and would not need her services until he got back in touch with her. When I thought back, that was exactly when I had begun to feel that something had happened to my old teacher. Anyway, then I had a lead."

"And how did that lead to your capture?" insisted Mrs. Zimmermann.

Uncle Jonathan grinned. "I'm getting to that, Florence! Well, I'm afraid I broke the law next, because I went over to Dr. Marville's house—I'd been there once already, but no one answered the doorbell, of course—and found a way to slip the lock on the back door. It looked as if a tornado had ripped through the place! Obviously once my late unlamented magical classmate had made sure no one would interrupt him, he had returned to ransack the house. I found this." Uncle Jonathan reached into his pants pocket and produced a thin piece of wood, one end badly splintered.

"Dr. Marville's wand?" asked Lewis.

"I think so—the very tip of it, anyway. The rest was just a scattering of splinters." Uncle Jonathan sighed. "I suspected then that Schlectesherz had really and truly done away with Dr. Marville. The only other times I've seen a wand explode like that have been when a magician was desperately trying to defend himself—and failed.

"Anyway, I drove back to New Zebedee after dark, thanking my lucky stars that I'd asked Florence to put those protective spells on Castle Barnavelt. I remember that I'd just pulled the car into the garage when I heard—I *thought* I heard—Lewis call out, 'Help!' I rushed out, and right into a spell that a shadowy figure had just fired at me, and the next thing I knew, I was in La-La Land, with the spirit of my old teacher drifting nearby. If it hadn't been for his encouragement, I might have floated completely away from the earth forever."

"What did Dr. Marville tell you?" asked Lewis.

Uncle Jonathan's expression became grim. "Dr. Marville told me of how Schlectesherz had spent his life gaining more and more magic power. Once some outraged citizens tried to lynch him, but they failed."

Lewis said, "Hal told me once he had fallen off a scaffold."

"Not Hal, but his master. That was old Schlectesherz talking through his dummy, like the ventriloquist Edgar Bergen speaks for Charlie McCarthy. Anyway, Dr. Marville let me know that Schlectesherz had attacked him and had destroyed his body—but his spirit was lingering behind in that misty halfway dimension, desperately trying to help us. Dr. Marville had tried to break through to our world in spectral form to warn me of the danger, but he could not manage to hold his shape for very long at all, and he could only briefly manifest close to where Schlectesherz and Hal happened to be. I suspect that is because Schlectesherz used the magic he stole from Dr. Marville to create Hal in the first place, so the doc could still call on it in a limited way. That was why Lewis glimpsed him for a second at the party and then later Rose Rita saw him down on the athletic field. However, Dr. Marville eventually learned that he could project a stronger image of himself into our magical hall mirror. That was why Lewis saw him there! And the number three that he kept sending was supposed to make me think of the third member of our group, old Adolfus. You see, we had a kind of silly rule that Doc Marville had adopted from the Golden Circle. The teacher calls himself One, his first pupil is Two—that was me—and the other pupil is Three. I should have made the connection, but I honestly thought the figure in the mirror was some evil force, and it never occurred to me that it was One trying to tell Two about Three!"

"So Dr. Marville was a good guy?" asked Lewis.

"He was one of the very best," said Uncle Jonathan quietly. He fished a bandanna from his pocket and loudly blew his nose. "Anyway, Dr. Marville let me know that Schlectesherz was frantically trying to get into my house to find the last thing that the two of us did together magically—our senior project. Since Adolfus did not receive his wand, he had no claim to it. He wanted it, though! He'd already picked up enough magic to create that foul hollow puppet he called Hal. Lord only knows what his ambitions were! To resurrect the German Reich, maybe, or to turn everyone into his slaves and minions. If he'd laid hands on our senior project, he might just have been on his way."

"What did you do?" asked Rose Rita.

Uncle Jonathan smiled. "Dr. Marville had been a teacher all his life. In that oddball spirit world, he continued to teach me. I learned how to make contact—just the briefest flicker at first—with my house. I could vaguely see through the enchanted stained-glass windows. And then I did the hardest magical feat I have ever performed in my life: I pulled all of

161

my own magic, every single solitary particle of it, right out of the house and into whatever existence I had in that twilight world. I suspected that once he unmade our mirror, old Schlectesherz was planning something awful for me, maybe intending to break my cane and leave me trapped forever, or maybe pull me back to earth and destroy me in a magical duel, so I needed all my strength. Then in the darkness I sensed something happening. I felt the change in the atmosphere when Schlectesherz cast his evil spell over my house—*my house*! But even so I couldn't find my way back again!"

"Until we bluffed Schlectesherz. It's a good thing he didn't stop to realize that inside a house over which he had cast spells, my magic was absolutely useless!"

"But the mirror was flashing red," said Lewis.

With a wink, Mrs. Zimmermann said, "Not by magic! We found your red flashlight, and I used that to fake a magical glow in the looking glass—and then Rose Rita put a high, hard fastball right across the plate and broke the mirror. That gave you time to smash the evil magician's wand!"

Uncle Jonathan nodded. "And the moment his wand broke, I saw a kind of doorway glimmering into existence right in front of me, and the spirit of Dr. Marville told me 'Go!' And the rest you know."

"It was my fault Hal got inside, and I helped him cast his spell," said Lewis. "I'm sorry."

"He tricked you," replied Uncle Jonathan. "And you were trying to help me. I'm proud of you, Lewis."

"What really happened to Hal?" asked Rose Rita.

With a sigh, Uncle Jonathan said, "There never was a real Hal. He was just an empty shell, manipulated by magic. I've checked with the school authorities, by the way. They have no record of Hal's ever being in New Zebedee—and I'll bet that even his teachers don't remember him now. All part of the magic."

"Hey," said Rose Rita. "That means I won the history medal!"

"Schlectesherz is really gone?" asked Lewis.

"For good, Lewis, thanks to you. Without his wand, he didn't have a hope. The tear in space and time vacuumed him up and sent his spirit packing. He won't be able to come back in any shape, form, or fashion."

"How do you know?" asked Rose Rita. "Can't he come back like Dr. Marville?"

"No," said Uncle Jonathan firmly. "Because his spirit has been called to its eternal reward, which I am afraid will not be a very nice one."

Mrs. Zimmermann said, "I am sorry, Weird Beard, for breaking your magical mirror. But why didn't that steal all your power away?"

"Oh, there's a pretty good reason, Pruny Face. I'll show you!" Uncle Jonathan got up and walked out of the room. A minute later he returned with a blobby, splotchy painting of a pinto horse, the one Lewis had noticed in his uncle's bedroom when he and Hal had been searching. It looked like a paint-by-numbers picture, done by someone without any talent, or even the ability to read numbers. He also had a small can of turpentine and a handful of rags. "Watch this," he said. He began to scrub at the paint, and it melted away, revealing a bright square of glass.

"A mirror?" asked Lewis.

"*The* mirror," corrected his uncle with a conspiratorial wink. "The one that belongs in the coat stand in the hall. You see, I have a confession to make: After you had gone to bed the night before my trip, I took a square mirror of about the right size from an antique wash-stand up on the third floor and substituted it for the real one in the coat stand. I spent a lot of the night before I was going to search for Dr. Marville painting my horsie picture on the real one, just to disguise it. Then I stuck it in a crummy old frame and hung it on my wall. By then I had started to think that maybe my old college chum Schlectesherz might just be behind it all, and if he was—"

"Then the magic mirror was what old what's-his-face would come looking for!" said Rose Rita triumphantly.

"A-plus!" said Uncle Jonathan. "All right, this is clean enough. Come with me!"

In the front hall, Uncle Jonathan tugged the heavy

coat stand away from the wall, and going to work with a screwdriver, he soon had removed the old, broken mirror. He replaced it with the now-gleaming one he had disguised as a painting, re-set the screws, and then pushed the stand back into place.

"Viola!" he said, making Mrs. Zimmermann wince.

"He means *voila*!" she said in a grumpy voice. "Which means, 'Hey, everybody, look at me!'"

"No—look at my old friend. So long, Doc," murmured Uncle Jonathan softly and sadly.

In the mirror, the robed figure floated in air beneath a blue sky. It threw them all a salute, and then magically transformed into a white dove that rose into the clear sky. A moment later, the mirror showed only their faces.

"He's gone," Mrs. Zimmermann said. "May he rest in peace."

"Amen to that," returned Uncle Jonathan.

"Will the mirror still be magic?" asked Lewis anxiously.

"You bet it will, nephew. It has no special significance—it was just a thingamabob that would demonstrate our magic power by tuning into exotic dimensions and places. Now it will be more magical than ever because the bad influences lingering on it from the time when it was made have now gone away. I expect—"

The phone rang, and Jonathan went to answer it. He

had a short conversation and then came back looking smug. "Well, well, well," he said. "That was His Honor Sam Parker, the mayor of New Zebedee himself!"

Lewis said, "Oh, gosh! Maybe you're still in trouble! I forgot to tell you—he called and left a message."

Uncle Jonathan waved a hand. "Don't worry about it, Lewis, no harm done. And no, I am *not* in trouble! In fact, it's the other way around—the town has got itself into a pickle, and guess who's going to get it out?"

"What's going on?" asked Mrs. Zimmermann suspiciously.

"Wait and see," retorted Uncle Jonathan with an air of mystery. "And I hope after I pull this wonder off, you'll realize what a great man you've had living next door to you all these years!"

He wouldn't even tell Lewis what was up. But he chased them all out of his study that afternoon and emerged from it only at twilight, clutching his cane. "Come on!" he ordered. "Haggy, go get your umbrella!"

They all piled into the Muggins Simoon and careened down to the athletic field, where quite a crowd had gathered. The mayor came hurrying up. "Thank heavens!" he said. "My nephew says you did a wonderful display when you threw your party, and when we didn't get our shipment—are you ready, Jonathan?"

166

"Ready, Your Honor," said Jonathan smartly. "I've, uh, set everything up down past the trees there. Keep everyone away from the work area! We don't want any accidents."

"No, no, of course not! Thank you!"

"Follow me!" said Uncle Jonathan as Mayor Parker hurried back to the speaker's stand that had been set up in front of the bleachers. He strode purposefully across the field, toward the dark line of trees where Rose Rita had once glimpsed the floating hooded figure.

They passed through the trees and emerged in a broad clearing near the railroad tracks. "Okay," said Uncle Jonathan. "Here's the deal: Because a shipping company made a bad mistake, the Fourth of July fireworks were not delivered this afternoon. And the mayor thinks I have my own private store—that's why the whole town was gossiping about my magic show, Frizzy Wig! They wanted me to help out with the display this year, and now I've agreed to give the town a fireworks extravaganza."

Mrs. Zimmermann grinned. She held out her umbrella, and it immediately elongated into her magical staff. "Ready, Frazzle Face?"

"Ladies first, Prunella!"

Lewis gasped as a brilliant purple streak burst from the tip of Mrs. Zimmermann's cane, rose impossibly high, trailing a luminous, sinuous tail behind it, and at last burst into a million shooting stars. He heard the distant crowd gasp, "Ahhhh!"

"Watch this!" boomed Uncle Jonathan. He raised his cane, and from it shot a half-dozen silver rockets, screaming up into the dark sky to burst in showers of red, green, gold, blue, and yellow streamers.

"Oh, yeah?" asked Mrs. Zimmermann. "Hold on to your hat!" She fired off a hundred graceful spiraling sparks that transformed as they rose into pale purple pulsing forms like neon jellyfish.

"Try this one on for size!" laughed Uncle Jonathan.

Rose Rita tugged at Lewis's sleeve. "We might as well sit down and enjoy it," she said as a red, white, and blue American eagle made of fireworks flapped its wings and soared higher and higher.

The show went on for hours, and later everyone in New Zebedee said it was the best Fourth of July ever. And Lewis, who knew how much he had almost lost and how grateful he was to have his uncle back, wholeheartedly agreed.